The Irish Theatre Series 6
Edited by Robert Hogan, James Kilroy *and* Liam Miller

The Modern Irish Drama, *a documentary history*
I: The Irish Literary Theatre 1899-1901

The Modern Irish Drama
a documentary history I

The Irish Literary Theatre
1899-1901
by Robert Hogan and James Kilroy

The Dolmen Press

Humanities Press Inc.

Set in Times Roman type and printed
and published in the Republic of Ireland
by The Dolmen Press Limited
North Richmond Industrial Estate, North Richmond Street, Dublin 1

Distributed outside Ireland, except in the United States of America
and in Canada, by Oxford University Press.

Published in the United States of America and in Canada
by Humanities Press Inc.,
171 First Avenue, Atlantic Highlands, N.J. 07716

First published 1975

HARDBACK EDITION
ISBN 0 85105 222 3 : The Dolmen Press
ISBN 0-391-00377-1 : Humanities Press Inc.

PAPERBACK EDITION
ISBN 0 85105 274 6 : The Dolmen Press
ISBN 0-391-00378-X : Humanities Press Inc.

Contents

Acknowledgements   *page* 6

Introduction   7

1899   8

1900   61

1901   89

Appendix I: A list of first productions and first publications   131

Appendix II: *The Coming of Conaill*, in Irish and in English   137

Notes   145

Acknowledgements

Grateful acknowledgement is made to:

Ernest Benn, Ltd., for quotations from F. R. Benson, *My Memoirs*.

Srimati Rukmini Devi, for quotations from *We Two Together* and manuscripts by James Cousins.

J. M. Dent & Sons, Ltd., for quotation from W. H. Reed, *Elgar*.

Faber & Faber, Ltd., for quotation from 'The Day of Rabblement' in *Critical Writings of James Joyce*.

Stephen Fay, for quotations from the writings of F. J. Fay.

Nevin Griffith, for quotations from *The United Irishman*, and writings of Arthur Griffith.

Harcourt, Brace & World, Inc. for quotations from W. G. Fay and Catherine Carswell, *The Fays of the Abbey Theatre*.

Rupert Hart-Davis, Ltd., for quotations from Max Beerbohm, *Around Theatres*.

William Heinemann, Ltd., for quotations from Max Beerbohm, 'In Dublin'.

The Irish Independent, for quotations from *The Daily Nation, The Freeman's Journal* and *The Irish Daily Independent*.

The Irish Times, for quotations from *The Daily Express, The Dublin Evening Mail* and *The Irish Times*.

Gerald MacDermott, for quotations from the journals of Joseph Holloway.

The Society of Authors, for the Estate of Bernard Shaw, for quotations from the writings of G. B. Shaw.

A. P. Watt & Son, for quotations from W. B. Yeats, *Letters*.

The National Library of Ireland, for quotations from manuscript collection.

Percy M. Young, for quotations from *Elgar*.

Introduction

In this history, we have attempted to recreate something of the immediacy felt by those writers and actors and playgoers who, in the years from 1899 to 1901, were laying the foundations of a national drama for Ireland. Most histories, quite properly, are compilations of fact and assessments of value, and so also, we hope, is this one. Nevertheless, we have attempted to do more than set down a judicious appraisal of what happened. There are several such accounts, although none, we believe, so full and accurate as we have tried to make this one. Here, we have primarily attempted to recreate a sense of how it was at the moment, and to achieve this feeling of immediacy we have allowed the story to be told as much as possible by the people who were involved in it. W. B. Yeats, George Moore, Frank Fay have been our collaborators, and we have made great use of contemporary documents — of letters, memoirs, and forgotten newspaper accounts and reviews.

Perhaps more than most historians, the chronicler of the theatre is always thwarted by the fact of time. A theatrical performance exists for the moment, and even the vivid memories of those who saw a play are but dim and distorted reflections of the lost reality. How Burbage sounded, how Garrick looked, whatever was so inimitable about Nell Gwynn or Mrs. Siddons or Molly Allgood — these matters of purely visual or aural appeal are central to a great player's genius, and yet so rarely, so vaguely recorded.

We have attempted, then, to reconstruct what still can be reconstructed of the actuality and the excitement of these formative years in Dublin, when a new drama was being created from nothing. It is particularly appropriate that we allow the principals to tell the story largely in their own words, for the principals included people like Yeats, Moore, John Synge, the Fay brothers, Arthur Griffith, Joseph Holloway, Lady Gregory, Douglas Hyde, Miss Horniman, and Maud Gonne. The intrigues, the quarrels, the problems, as well as the wit, the humour, and the charm reside in their own words far more than they could in any paraphrase of ours.

ROBERT HOGAN
JAMES KILROY

1899

The centuries-long struggle of Ireland for its national independence was not an ever-growing movement whose final cumulative intensity was the 1916 Rising. Over the centuries, Irish nationalism has risen to many waves of intensity between many troughs of despair. One such intense movement reached its peak in 1890 under the inspiring leadership of Charles Stewart Parnell. When Parnell lost the leadership of the Irish party and then, in 1891, died struggling to regain it, the cause of Irish freedom received a reversal from which it did not recover for years. But, as Edmund Curtis remarked, 'in the grand disillusionment that followed Parnell the national cause took new and deeper channels than mere politics.' [1] One such channel was the intensification of an already growing movement in literature. It was a movement which looked directly to Ireland, to Irish legend and Irish history, for its inspiration. It was a movement which was abruptly to blossom into what has been justly called the Irish Renaissance.

There had been, of course, Irish writers before the 1890's who had written about Ireland. Maria Edgeworth and William Carleton had both taken Ireland for their subject, but both in different ways had not quite attained what Lennox Robinson was to call 'this Irish thing'. Maria Edgeworth, for all her knowledge, was an outsider painting with sympathy, but with an outsider's incomplete understanding. Carleton, the son of a peasant, did know intimately what he was writing about, but he grafted an alien style onto his subject, thus exaggerating and distorting it. Similarly, the fervent patriotic poems of the Young Ireland group suffered as much from English poetic diction as they did from their authors' minor talents. However, with the poems of James Clarence Mangan and Sir Samuel Ferguson, and perhaps even with the flawed novels of Charles J. Kickham, the first indications of an Irish literature that was both Irish and literature began to appear.

Ernest Boyd dates the true beginnings of modern Irish literature with the publication of two volumes by Standish O'Grady: his *History of Ireland : The Heroic Period* in 1878, and his *History of Ireland : Cuculain and his Contemporaries* in 1880. These volumes were an exultant celebration of Irish legendary materials, and, although in prose, were vibrant with poetic fervour. As Æ wrote in

8

1902, 'Years ago, in the adventurous youth of his mind, Mr. O'Grady found the Gaelic tradition like a neglected antique dún with the doors barred. Listening, he heard from within the hum of an immense chivalry, and he opened the doors and the wild riders went forth to work their will.' [2] To this, W. B. Yeats added the footnote that, 'I think it was his *History of Ireland, Heroic Period*, that started us all. . . .' [3]

What it had started was this: In 1888 the Dublin firm of M. H. Gill and Son published *Poems and Ballads of Young Ireland*, which included the work of most of the new poets — Yeats, T. W. Rolleston, John Todhunter, Katherine Tynan, Rose Kavanagh, and others — and which, according to Boyd, 'announced the co-operative, concerted nature of the effort of the younger generation to give a new impulse to Irish poety'. [4] In 1899, Yeats published *The Wanderings of Oisin*. In 1891, at a meeting at Yeats's house in London, he, Rolleston, Todhunter, and others initiated what was to become in the next year the Irish Literary Society of London. Also in 1892, a sister organization, the National Literary Society, was formed in Dublin, and Douglas Hyde gave before it his influential lecture on 'The Necessity for De-Anglicising Ireland'. In that same year Yeats published his play *The Countess Cathleen*. In 1893, Hyde published his beautiful *The Love Songs of Connacht* and founded the Gaelic League for the propagation of the Irish language. In 1893 also, Yeats's volume *The Celtic Twilight* gave a descriptive tag to the whole movement. In the next year he published another play, *The Land of Heart's Desire*, and it was produced in March in London together with Todhunter's *A Comedy of Sighs*. In 1897, George Sigerson published his *Bards of the Gael and Gall*. In 1899, Hyde published his monumental *Literary History of Ireland*. And in 1899, the Irish Literary Theatre made its first appearance.

*   *   *

The originality of the Irish Literary Theatre in 1899 can probably best be appreciated by a knowledge of what the other Dublin theatres were doing.

The New Theatre Royal had been originally opened in January, 1821, and on that occasion Colman the Younger wrote an opening address which began:

Hail, generous Natives of Green Erin's Isle;
Welcome, kind Patrons, to our new-rais'd Pile.

After noting that all of the labour on the new building had been
done by Irishmen, he briefly charted the history of the site.

Here once a Market reared its busy head,
Where sheep, instead of tragic heroes, bled;
Bright cleavers form'd a band to charm the ears;
Joints dangled in the place of Chandeliers.
Stout Butchers, stern as Critics, had their day,
And cut up oxen, like a modern Play.
Soon Science came; — his steel the Butcher drops,
Removes, with awe, the shambles and the shops,
And Learning triumphed over Mutton Chops![5]

Although Colman's verses will never rank among the flowers of
English poetry, they seem masterly indeed when compared to the
address written by Edwin Hamilton, Esq. on the occasion of the
re-opening of the theatre after restoration on 13 December 1897.
In charting the theatre's history, Hamilton wrote:

Here, in sublime, soul-stirring, stately scenes,
Appeared Charles Young, the Kembles, and the Keans,
Macready, Brooke, bright stars of long ago;
Here — in his line unrivalled — Boucicault:
Then — loved as player, patriot, and man —
Our home-born genius, Barry Sullivan.[6]

No home-born genius was to tread the boards of the new Royal
under the directorship of H. H. Morrell and Frederick Mouillot,
for the theatre depended almost entirely upon English touring companies doing light drama and comedy. Some typical productions
of 1898 and 1899 were George Alexander's Company with Scenery,
Furniture and Effects from the St. James's Theatre, London, in
The Man of Forty by Walter Frith, in which Alexander was supported by H. B. Irving and C. Aubrey Smith; the celebrated actress,
Miss Annie Hughes, Mr. Edmund Maurice and Company in Robert
Buchanan's comedy *Sweet Nancy*; Mrs. Brown Potter and Mr.

Kyrle Bellew supported by their London company in Bulwer-Lytton's *The Lady of Lyons* and *Camille* of Dumas *fils*; Mr. J. L. Shine, supported by the Globe Theatre, London, Company, in an original play entitled *An Irish Gentleman* by David Christie Murray and Shine; George and Weedon Grossmith in *Young Mr. Yarde*, a farce by Harrold Ellis and Paul A. Rubens. There were many productions of light operas, such as *The Bohemian Girl, The Daughter of the Regiment* and *The Lily of Killarney* by travelling groups like the Moody Manners Opera Company. There were also many musical comedies, such as the popular *The Belle of New York, Little Miss Nobody, Topsy-Turvey Hotel, The Skirt Dancer, A Greek Slave* and *The Squatter's Daughter*. Occasionally there was the spectacular melodrama, which still had not quite gone out of style, such as that 'Up-to-date Drury Lane Sporting Drama' *The Prodigal Daughter* by Henry Pettitt and Sir Augustus Harris, 'with all the Original Drury Lane Scenes, Dresses, and 6 Blood Horses including the Grand National Winner VOLUPTUARY.' And not at all infrequently there was even an accomplished artist in an interesting, if un-Irish play. Mrs. Patrick Campbell played at the Royal in *The Second Mrs. Tanqueray, The Notorious Mrs. Ebbsmith* and *Magda*. Julia Neilson, Louis Calvert, William Mollison and Lillian Braithwaite appeared in *As You Like It*. The Benson Company, with such fine actors as Oscar Asche and Frank Rodney, appeared in *Antony and Cleopatra* and *The School for Scandal*. Winifred Emery and Cyril Maude appeared in Barrie's *The Little Minister*, and Martin Harvey appeared in *The Only Way*, the popular adaptation of *A Tale of Two Cities*.

However, about the only nod to Irish drama given by the Royal was a run in July, 1899, by E. C. Matthews' Company of Boucicault's *Arrah-na-Pogue* and *The Colleen Bawn*. Frank Fay, reviewing the plays in *The United Irishman*, greeted them with only faint praise:

> For the stuff that ordinarily goes by the name of "Irish Drama", the company would probably be quite adequate. But, with the exception of Mr. Somerfield Arnold, it does not contain anyone who, by even a stretch of imagination, could be called an artist; and if we are to feel the poetry, the laughter, mingled with tears, so predominant in the Irish character, we must have Boucicault's Irish plays interpreted by *artists*. When

11

the managers of the Scotch theatres revive, as they do each year, *Rob Roy* (Pocock's miserable travesty of the novel), *Jeannie Deans* (another of Boucicault's plays, by the way), *The Lady of the Lake*, &c., they engage artists of the calibre of William Mollison, so well known to Dublin playgoers as a Shakespearian actor. Except Ada Rehan, there is not, unfortunately, a single Irish dramatic artist of the first rank at present on the stage, and she is Irish by birth only; therefore we cannot hope to see worthy revivals of Irish plays by first-class Irish artists. But when we go to the Theatre Royal, which poses as a first-class house, to see Irish Drama, we have every right to expect to find the best Irish talent available in the cast. Why is not that admirable and versatile actor, Mr. Frank Dalton, in the cast? Where is his sister, Mrs. Charles Sullivan? Where is Mr. Tom Nerney (so long associated with Boucicault)? I suppose Mr. E. C. Matthews is the best Irish comedian to be had at present, but as Shaun he is only passable. Like his kind and doubtless because he plays more often in England than in Ireland, he "plays for the laugh" all the time, and the audience punish him by laughing at his pathos, and this is exasperating to one who considers that their poetry, pathos and tenderness are the only qualities which distinguish *The Colleen Bawn*, *The Shaughraun* and *Arrah-na-Pogue* from ordinary melodrama.[7]

In another review, Fay scored the audience as much as the players:

A very large audience assembled in the popular portions of the house to witness the performance, but with regret, I find myself compelled to say that the majority of them seemed to be of the intensely uncritical and ignorant type, only too common in Dublin, the class who will madly applaud a singer or an instrumentalist, no matter how much out of tune the former may sing or how wretchedly the latter may play, provided they finish with the conventional bluster. That they were noisy and ill-behaved is nothing, because one does not expect much from such people; but that they should scream with boorish laughter, when one of the characters in the play spoke a few words of Irish, will scarcely be credited by anyone who was not present.[8]

12

Fay found little of Irish interest to intrigue him at Dublin's other first-class house, the Gaiety, which from 27 December 1897 to 1 May 1909 was managed by the Gunn family. As with the Royal, there was practically never during this entire period a programme at the Gaiety that was about Ireland or that used local talent. This theatre also depended chiefly on English touring companies, bringing the latest farce or melodrama to the provinces. Occasionally a great actor or actress, such as Coquelin or Bernhardt, would appear briefly; and occasionally an accomplished touring company, such as F. R. Benson's or Edward Compton's, would appear in Shakespeare or the classic English comedies. But for the most part, the Gaiety, like the Royal, was given over to crowd-pleasing entertainments.

In 1899, for example, the D'Oyly Carte appeared twice: in February and again in November. The George Edwardes Company was featured three times during the year, playing *A Runaway Girl* two of the times. The always popular *Charley's Aunt*[9] would run for one week, followed by Sardou's *La Tosca* the next. On 17 April, Thomas E. Murray's Company opened in a play called *Our Irish Visitors*. Murray was an Irish-American comedian whose 'primitive funniments and outlandish dialect' Bernard Shaw had once found mildly amusing, although they smacked to him more 'of the village rather than of the West End. But he is imperturbably good-humoured, sings in tune, and surprises the audience into laughing at his childlike jokes several times on which scores much is forgiven him.'[10] *Our Irish Visitors* was not an Irish but an American farcical comedy, and its pretensions are adequately described in the Gaiety advertisement: 'Constructed for Laughing Purposes Only. 180 Laughs in 180 Minutes!' Henry Arthur Jones's *The Manoeuvres of Jane* and several plays by Arthur Wing Pinero were presented in the spring; and on 23 June, Coquelin and his company played in French Rostand's *Cyrano de Bergerac* and, on the following day, *Tartuffe* and *Les Précieuses Ridicules*. On 2 October, Mrs. Lewis Waller and her London Company, including Mr. Robert Loraine and Miss Mary Rorke, appeared in *The Three Musketeers*. Mrs. Waller was, of course, the wife of the reigning matinee idol of the English stage. Rather more interesting than the romantic heroics of Dumas was the company's other presentation, James B. Fagan's *The Rebels*, described as 'A New Romantic Irish Play', and with H. B. Warner in the cast. Fagan in later years was to write some

13

extremely popular plays and to have a distinguished career in London as a producer of both continental masterpieces and Irish dramas. *The Rebels* was Fagan's first play, and unfortunately appears not to have been published.[11] In December, the Compton Company played its usual repertoire of Sheridan, Goldsmith and some new plays. And on Boxing Day the pantomime opened as usual, this year's being *Little Red Riding Hood*.

One other theatre was licensed to present plays. This was a second-class house, The Queen's Royal Theatre — or, as it was usually called, The Queen's. At this time the theatre was managed by J. W. Whitbread, an Englishman who was writing a number of popular, very broad and very bad, neo-Boucicaultian melodramas. In the 1890's, the Queen's was given over either to the production of patriotic pieces *à la* Boucicault or to the production of old-fashioned, but still popular, spectacular melodramas. Both the quality of the plays and of the productions was considerably lower than what might be seen at the Theatre Royal or at the Gaiety.

A typical Queen's melodrama of the period was *The Bandit King,* which the indefatigable playgoer Joseph Holloway saw on the evening of 24 September 1895. It was, he wrote:

> . . . a drama written round four trained horses. Mr. J. H. Wallick took the part of "Jesse James", the outlaw, and although he has been playing it for fifteen years he struck me as not being up to much as a melodramatic actor. . . . The other parts were indifferently filled. The piece was rot. The house was full. There was so much shooting during the unfolding of the incidents, that you would at times imagine you were at a "field day" in the Fifteen Acres in the Park.[12]

On 15 September 1896 Holloway went to the Queen's, and saw

> . . . a noisy, rough-and-tumble, song and dance, American sensational play, entitled *One of the Bravest*, with a realistic fire scene, including fire engine, etc., complete. The play, in fact, seemed to have been written round this tableau. The piece, like most American dramas, has no plot to speak of, and plenty of knockabout, grotesque characters.[13]

On 6 October Holloway saw one of the few pieces at the Queen's with any pretentions to literature, Charles Reade's *Drink*, an adaptation of Zola's *L'Assommoir*. Charles Warner had made a minor reputation playing the lead, and his death scene seems to have been in the best tradition of nineteenth century melodramatic acting. 'The shattered wreck of humanity, foaming at the mouth and almost tearing himself to pieces in his frenzy, will always remain a nightmare recollection in my mind,' remarked Holloway, who was impressed even by the scenery and reported that the fall from the scaffold in Act 4 caused many of the audience to cry out, 'My God, is he killed!' [14]

The Queen's audience demanded strong situations, and the play which Holloway saw there on 4 May 1897, certainly provided them. The piece was *The Trail of the Serpent* by F. Marriot Watson, and Holloway remarked that the scene in the smelting works 'was intensely realistic, and a thrill of fear passed through the house as the lever bearing the fainting form of the heroine moved towards the furnace to deposit her therein. It was certainly admirably managed, and her rescue in the nick of time was a great relief to all.' [15] On 29 June Holloway saw a Western Romance by Fred Darcy entitled *The New World*, which he described as 'a most interesting, exciting well-made drama of its class, with endless pistol-shooting, knife-flashing, hair-breadth escapes, lynching songs, dances, and fun.' He was particularly impressed by the lynching scene in Act 1, in which 'the man was actually dangling in mid-air before the rope was shot in twain above him.' [16] On 9 November, he saw a play called *Shaft No. 2*, 'the first drama that has been written around electricity which we have seen in Dublin.' The highpoint of the drama was 'a realistic representation of one on the point of being put death in an electrocution chair.' [17]

On 21 December he saw Mr. Herbert Barr's Company play George Gray's four-act drama, *The Football King*, a piece whose myriad excitements are worth describing at some length:

The novelty round which the piece is written . . . is an Association Football Match — the final for the English Cup at Kennington Oval — played in full view of the audience with cheering multitude of small boys, goal posts, and all — an exciting episode as the ball was twice kicked across the footlights into the pit despite the netting placed almost across the stage between the audience and the players. The general shindy at the end of the match was realistic as well as amusing. The whole bag of tricks of melodrama was used in the construction

15

of the work, and the hero was as loud-voiced, declamatory, and spotless as they make them, while the villain would stop at nothing, and committed murders, poisoned, seduced, and abducted every other minute for the mere fun of the thing, it would seem. And, of course, he was well-dressed, deep-voiced, long-haired, black-moustached and eyebrowed, and smoked cigarettes beyond counting. One of the most amusing incidents occurred in Act 4, Scene 3, where the villain places his discarded mistress on the rails in an insensible[18] condition as the train is approaching, and she is supposed to be rescued by the hero in the nick of time. The hero on this occasion being a moment late had to forceably stop the train with his strong right hand in order to take the lady out of harm's way.[19]

On 3 August 1898 Holloway saw *The Terror of Paris* by E. Hill-Mitchelson and Charles H. Longdon, and was much thrilled by the scene 'in the Glassworks at St. Cloud, when the spy "Laroche" is denounced, and his eyes are about to be gouged out with molten glass from the furnaces. . . .'[20] On 9 August he saw Mr. John H. Preston's Company in an Oriental drama by Max Goldberg, entitled *The Secrets of the Harem, or The Cross and the Crescent*. The plot is the usual involved and thrilling hokum about a beautiful Christian girl caught in the toils of a lustful Pasha and rescued by the brave young Englishman, Lieutenant Herbert Markman, R.N. From the point of view of the emerging Irish drama, the scene in which the heroine is being sold at the slave auction is of some interest. As Holloway described it:

> The Lieutenant is determined to purchase her, but is outbid by the sensual Pasha who is about to claim her when "Markman" draws the Union Jack around her and defies them in the name of his country to touch it. The curtain descending in a very effective tableau amid cheers from the audience. This was the first time I ever heard an Irish audience cheer the Union Jack, or English pluck on the stage.[21]

We can hardly leave this discussion of the Queen's spectacular melodrama without mentioning Charles Locksley's amazing drama *Humanity*, which Holloway saw John Lawson's Company perform on 3 November 1898. The play's advertisements boasted:

Such a dénouement never before witnessed on the British Stage. Complete wreckage and demolition of a magnificently furnished Drawing Room. Smashing of windows, pier glasses, statues, ornaments, and *the fight until death on the collapsing staircase!* The breakages alone amounting to a Star's salary.[22]

This, of course, was sheer delight for the Queen's audience, and Holloway reported that 'as each article came crashing down a cry of suppressed astonishment escaped the lips of most who witnessed this truly appalling scene of destruction.' The room was destroyed in a fight between the hero and the villain, and Mr. John Lawson, remarked Holloway, gave a remarkable impersonation of the hero— 'quiet and artistic, as well as realistic. . . .'

In addition to these spectacular melodramas, the Queen's produced the Irish plays of Boucicault and the patriotic melodramas which J. W. Whitbread was turning out according to the Boucicault formula. That formula — a mélange of thrills, laughter, pathos and patriotism — offered an exaggerated and unrealistically simple view of Ireland, and it was this kind of drama against which W. B. Yeats and his colleagues were to rebel. Their rebellion so successfully swept the stage-Irishman off the stage that it was not immediately apparent how several of the masterpieces of the new Irish drama — such as Synge's *The Playboy of the Western World,* O'Casey's *Juno and the Paycock,* M. J. Molloy's *The King of Friday's Men,* and Brendan Behan's *The Hostage* — owed a very considerable debt to the Boucicaultian melodrama. In the last five or ten years there has been a revival of interest in melodrama and even a re-appraisal of Boucicault. In the World Theatre Festival at the Aldwych Theatre, London, in May, 1968, the Abbey Theatre's entry was an enthusiastically received revival of Boucicault's *The Shaughraun,* and Ronald Bryden heralded that occasion with a perceptive and convincing defence of melodrama in *The Observer* Sunday magazine. The cycle of taste again seemed to have come full circle.

Whatever their intrinsic merits, the Boucicault melodramas at the Queen's were at best unevenly presented, and the bald Whitbread imitations intended to evoke only cheap thrills and easy laughter. In 1899 the time had almost passed for Irish melodrama. The form was shortly to receive a new injection of vitality from the movies, but to the playgoer it was beginning to seem old-fashioned. On 26

17

August 1899, Frank Fay reviewed a revival of Whitbread's *Wolfe Tone*, and his dissatisfaction is beginning to be apparent.

> Of the many plays written and produced at the Queen's Theatre by Mr. J. W. Whitbread, *Wolfe Tone*, his latest, is to my mind, his best. The theatre-going public were evidently of the same opinion, for the play continued to attract large audiences for a full month after its production on St. Stephen's Day, 1898. . . . We have not yet had a real historical Irish drama, and the author of *Wolfe Tone* cannot give us one, but with the skill born of long connection with and knowledge of the boards and of the class of audience to which he appeals, Mr. Whitbread has construced an exceedingly effective play, which he calls "A Romantic Irish Drama". It is really neither more nor less than a well-constructed melodrama. . . .[23]

Later in the year Fay wrote a much more caustic review of Whitbread's play, *The Irishman*:

> Each time I have seen it the play was interpreted by thoroughly competent players; but *The Irishman* remains a crude piece of unconvincing conventionalism, without any right to its name. Before the first act was half through, all my old friends, whom I never met outside melodramas, had made their appearance. . . . I positively loathe the virtuous persons of melodrama, and would have their blood were it not that, between us, intervenes that horrible instrument of torture, the orchestra of the Queen's theatre.[24]

Later in the month the Kennedy Miller Combination revived John Baldwin Buckstone's *The Green Bushes*, which had originally been produced in 1845, and Fay remarked that a large audience treated the old play with 'amusing toleration'. He concluded, 'I suppose the day of *The Green Bushes* is nearly over.'[25]

Of course, as the clientele of the Queen's was an undemanding one, which was easily delighted with simple characterization and broad effects, the acting tended to be, with some notable exceptions, rather slovenly exaggerations of a nineteenth century broad style. When Joseph Holloway went to the Queen's on 13 August 1895, to see Fred Cooke's company in Cooke's drama *On Shannon's Shore, or The Blackthorn*, he remarked:

18

Oh my! it was shockingly bad! Too absurd for anything! Mr. Fred Cooke, the author, behaved in the character of "Barney Shanaghan" as a blithering idiot right through and nearly made me ill by his exaggerated tomfoolery.[26]

It was, of course, the Boucicault productions at the Queen's that came closest to nature, and a more tolerant Holloway reminiscence may indicate how close, at best, the Queen's came to giving a realistic view of Ireland.

A typical Queen's audience, noisy and full of suggestions to the players, filled the cosy little theatre to see Dion Boucicault's admirably constructed and most interesting Irish drama, *Arrah-na-Pogue*, acted by Kennedy Miller's Favourite Company of Irish Players. The Queen's is the home of Irish drama. There you may always reckon to see this form of piece well played by genuinely Irish actors; and, as the audience knows every line of the text and every bit of by-play in the various parts, it sees that it gets the full value for its money, or lets those on the stage know why. Such genuine, innocent, hearty laughter as the racy dialogue and droll situations brought to life became so infectious that I had to join in the laughter myself. . . . A more uproariously funny scene, intermingled with pathos and patriotism, than the Court Martial Scene in Act 2 where poor "Séan the Post" is tried and condemned for the robbery of money from the process server, "Michael Feeny", or one better played all-round, is seldom seen.

And the Queen's stage seemed made for the wedding scene in the barn, as the gates at the rear of the stage only have to be opened to allow the cars to pass up the laneway, and one can see from the theatre the College wall and position of the College buildings in the dim light of the dark-black night outside. Nature forming a background to the stage picture! Instead of the noisy rattling of horses' hoofs on the boards, they drive up the natural road of the laneway and discharge their load right onto the back of the stage in the most natural way possible, and when big Kitty Walsh arrived on her private ass and cart, there was a roar of delight from the house.[27]

19

But despite the pleasure that Fay and Holloway could still derive from Boucicault, if not from his imitators, the acting was usually overdone and sometimes outrageously false. What was happening at the Queen's was the last twitch of a dying convention. A new drama which would truly reflect contemporary Ireland would have to be different and would have to be acted differently.

* * *

To round out the picture of the Dublin stage at the end of the last century, it should be mentioned that the city had one or two variety houses, which seldom or never included dramatic pieces on their bills. The most popular, and a still functioning theatre, was the one which is now called the Olympia in Dame Street. In 1896 the theatre had been called Dan Lowrey's Star Theatre of Varieties, but in 1897 its name was changed to the Empire Palace Theatre. Its Grand Opening Programme of Monday, 15 November 1897, is a quite typical one:

1 Overture, "Rosamunde", Schubert.
2 Mr. Lester King, Character Baritone Vocalist.
3 Celest, Novelty Wire Act.
4 Miss Dulcie Laing, Contralto Vocalist and Dancer.
5 Virto, the Man of Many Instruments.
6 Griff, Comic Juggler.
7 Werner & Rieder, Duettists and Swiss Warblers.
8 Frantz Family, Lady and Gentlemen Acrobats.

Interval of 10 Minutes

9 Selection, *Maritana*, Wallace.
10 Miss Florence Esdaile, Australian Soprano Vocalist.
11 Lumiere Triograph, With Special Local Views, &c.
12 Charles Coborn, Favourite Comedian and Vocalist.
13 Eight Eldorados, Vocalists and Expert Dancers.
14 Morris and Morris, American Acrobatic Grotesques.[28]

In 1898 and 1899, the theatre billed such attractions as Zaro and Arno, 'The Heathen Chinee', in their Great Horizontal Bar Act; Minnie Ray, Champion Lady Clog Dancer of the World; Professor

Vox, the popular singing Ventriloquist; and Franks' Roosters, a Novelty Act with Roosters, Dogs and Bantams. The bill at the Empire Palace was not greatly different from what was to be seen at the Lyric Theatre of Varieties, while in the Round Room of the Rotunda one was likely to see a home-grown concert show featuring Miss Clara Butt.

*   *   *

In his reviews in *The United Irishman*, Frank Fay was fond of pointing out that, 'In the last century we gave Quin, Macklin, Barry and Peg Woffington, Mossop and Sheridan (father and son) to the English stage. What has become of our histrionic ability? Is it that we lack the perseverance necessary?' [29]

There was, of course, still professional Irish acting and entertaining. Actors such as Chalmers Mackay, Frank Breen and Frank Dalton achieved some professional success, although none became widely known outside of Ireland. Mainly, the Irish professional actor played in Boucicault or imitations of Boucicault, and so offered nothing new to the development of an indigenously Irish style of acting. Mr. and Mrs. McHardy Flint conducted classes in acting in Dublin, and occasionally gave recitals which might include scenes from Shakespeare or the eighteenth century comic dramatists. Percy French could often be seen in his medley of songs, comic monologues and lightning sketches.

Frank Fay's brother, W. G., had a good deal of experience in fit-up companies. He toured Ireland and England with J. W. Lacy's Company, H. E. Bailey's Comedy Company, Lloyd's Mexican Circus, and even with what was probably the first production in Ireland of *Uncle Tom's Cabin* in a company headed by an American Negro actor, R. B. Lewis. Both the Fay brothers were hopelessly stagestruck, and from 1891 to 1903 they played in and around Dublin with their own amateur company, which was first called the Ormond Dramatic Society, and later W. G. Fay's Comedy Combination or W. G. Fay's Celebrated Variety Group. Some of the actors attracted to the group, such as Dudley Digges and Sara Allgood, were later to become famous, and of course several of them formed the nucleus of the Irish National Theatre Society.

In 1899 W. G. Fay had returned from his wanderings and taken a job as an electrician, and Frank was secretary to a firm of accountants, but their main energies were devoted to the production of plays in the evening. As W. G. Fay remarked, 'As we never put on any plays that took a full evening to perform, it was possible to have always on hand a programme of short plays, which demanded a minimum of rehearsal and gave us a reasonable chance of replacing actors who moved on to other things or left the town.' [30] The plays were nothing remarkable — *Box and Cox, His Last Legs, Paddy Miles' Boy, That Rascal Pat, The Irish Tutor, The Secret, Who Speaks First?* — and the programmes were usually filled out by poems, songs and recitations.[31]

Despite almost thirteen or fourteen years of experience, the productions of the Fays' amateur group should not be overestimated. As late as 3 December 1897, Joseph Holloway could view one of their performances and remark:

> The Ormond Dramatic Society gave a triple bill and concert in the Molesworth Hall before a large and friendly audience. The Society had a shot at Buckstone's comic drama, *A Rough Diamond*, and failed to score. Mr. C. William Crowe's "Sir William Evergreen" was chiefly noted for the vagaries of his moustache. Miss E. Knowles put on an antic disposition as "Margery", the untutored country lass who weds above her station, and everyone saw that she did. Her dialect was a mixture of Dublin accent and cold in the head. Mr. Frank Evelyn [F. J. Fay] was a colourless "Lord Plato" (his face, though, had on a liberal supply of colour). The one-act pieces, *The Limerick Boy* and *Advice Gratis*, were also played, but I had enough, thank you, for one evening.[32]

*   *   *

Despite the literary revival, a good deal of the original writing in Ireland continued for several years yet to imitate English models. Much of the popular fiction was a romantic or a melodramatic treatment of the English upper class. It is scarcely an exaggeration to say that, in such popular journals as *The Weekly Freeman* and *The Weekly Independent*, there were just two types of illustration for stories and serials. One type showed a moustachioed gentleman in evening dress either plaintively kneeling at the feet or deferentially bending over the hand of an imposing and rather large

22

maiden. The second type showed one moustachioed gentleman threatening to stab, shoot, or push over a cliff another moustachioed gentleman. George Fitzmaurice, who began his brilliant career with a series of comic stories of Irish life in these journals remarked satirically in one of his stories that the heroine

> from being an occasional purchaser had developed into a regular weekly reader of the *Family Speaker*, a periodical whose four serials were always written in the most highflown language, though now and then a little obscure in meaning. The contents were invariably devoted to depicting life in aristocratic circles, and it was an odd hero who was not a duke, a marquis, an earl, or at the very least a mere ordinary lord. The heroines in like manner were mostly "my ladys" or misses of high degree, and if a plebeian was now and then thrown in for the sake of contrast she was bound to change her state in due time by hooking a lord.[33]

What little dramatic writing there was also tended to be conventional imitation of English models. For instance, Mary Costello, a prolific writer of popular fiction, published in a woman's magazine, *The Lady of the House*, in 1893 and 1894 a play in two scenes called *The Tragedy of a Simple Soul*. Its nature may be inferred from its principal characters: the Hon. Edgar Haldane, Captain, Knightstream Guards; Miss Constance Pennefather and Miss Edith Pennefather; and Miss Nancy Hart, daughter of a bankrupt sporting squire. In the same magazine for the Christmas issue of 1900, Miss Costello published another short play called *A Daughter to Marry*. The characters included the Marquise De Montliva, who is described as an American heiress; Mrs. Harry B. Vandenhoff, her cousin; Claire De Montliva, her stepdaughter, described as a Convent Ingenue; and Captain Bodin, who wears a French uniform of the Line and has a deep sabre cut from eye to chin. The nature of the play may be inferred from the following sample of dialogue:

> CLAIRE   [*Sweeping past*]: At last you realise my sentiments, Monsieur. [*At door*] Your conduct inspires me with detestation. [*Exit*]
>
> CAPTAIN BODIN   [*In a fury*]: Criée nom d'un nom! What does it mean — this insult, this infamy? [*Pacing*

23

stage] If she were a man, a man! [*Gripping his sword*] How her eyes blazed, her voice quivered with contempt![34]

This, then, was the theatrical and literary background of Dublin in the year 1899. It was time for a new inspiration.

* * *

The idea of a literary theatre for Dublin originated with W. B. Yeats, and originally seemed a most incongruous notion. As George Moore put it, when Yeats and Edward Martyn first spoke to him of the project, 'to give a Literary Theatre to Dublin seemed to me like giving a mule a holiday. . . .'[35]

Yeats in the 1890's was an increasingly appreciated young poet who had always been interested in the theatre. Indeed, much of his juvenilia had been plays, and in an article published late in his life he wrote that he used to read his early dramatic poems to a school friend, Charles Johnston. 'I recall three plays,' he wrote, 'not of any merit, one vaguely Elizabethan, its scene a German forest, one an imitation of Shelley, its scene a crater in the moon, one of somebody's translation from the Sanscrit, its scene an Indian temple.'[36]

One of Yeats' very first published pieces was *The Island of Statues*, 'an Arcadian Faery Tale — in Two Acts', which was published in *The Dublin University Review* in the number of April-July, 1885. The same magazine published in its September, 1885, number *The Seeker*, 'a Dramatic Poem — in Two Scenes', and in the June, 1886, number *Mosada*, a dramatic poem. The last play, published separately later in the year, was Yeats's first book, and all three of these early pieces, with one other slight dramatic work, were included in Yeats's second book, *The Wanderings of Oisin*, published in 1889.

Yeats's first active experience of the stage came five years later when his play *The Land of Heart's Desire* was produced on 29 March 1894, at the Avenue Theatre, London. Florence Farr, a friend of his and an amateur actress of note, had, with financial backing from Miss A. E. F. Horniman, leased the theatre for a short season of plays, and Yeats's piece was a curtain raiser first to John Todhunter's *A Comedy of Sighs* and then to Bernard

Shaw's *Arms and the Man*. Yeats's biographer, Joseph Hone, described the first night as 'a complete disaster', but also remarked that, 'Yeats was in the theatre almost every night for several weeks, noting in the light of the performances the changes he might make in the monosyllabic verse, in which his interpreters were ill at ease.' [37]

In a letter describing the productions to John O'Leary, the old Fenian, Yeats wrote, 'The whole venture will be history anyway for it is the first contest between the old commercial school of theatrical folk and the new artistic school.' [38]

The idea of a literary theatre for Dublin now strongly began to take shape in Yeats's mind, and in 1897 he discussed the matter first with Lady Augusta Gregory and then with Edward Martyn. Lady Gregory and Martyn were near neighbours in the West of Ireland, and Martyn, a rich Catholic landlord, had already written two plays which had been offered unsuccessfully to an English actor-manager. Lady Gregory, the widow of an ex-Governor of Ceylon, had edited her husband's autobiography and was eager to help in the Literary Revival. The immediate result of their conversations was a letter signed by the three of them and sent to various prominent Irishmen. Part of it was quoted in Lady Gregory's *Our Irish Theatre*:

> We propose to have performed in Dublin, in the spring of every year certain Celtic and Irish plays, which whatever be their degree of excellence will be written with a high ambition, and so to build up a Celtic and Irish school of dramatic literature. We hope to find in Ireland an uncorrupted and imaginative audience trained to listen by its passion for oratory, and believe that our desire to bring upon the stage the deeper thoughts and emotions of Ireland will ensure for us a tolerant welcome, and that freedom to experiment which is not found in theatres of England, and without which no new movement in art or literature can succeed. We will show that Ireland is not the home of buffoonery and of easy sentiment, as it has been represented, but the home of an ancient idealism.[39]

The intention of the letter was to raise a guarantee of £300 for the production of plays in Dublin in the spring of the next three years. According to Lady Gregory, the response to the letter varied considerably, but the real setback was that the patent theatres in Dublin were too expensive, and that an old law prohibited theatrical performances for money in buildings not licensed for dramatic performance. However, with the help of W. E. H. Lecky and other Irish Members of Parliament, Yeats, Martyn and Lady Gregory succeeded in getting the law amended. Then Martyn applied to the Dublin Town Clerk for permission to give performances in May, 1899. To forestall opposition from the established theatres, Martyn emphasized the non-commercial nature of the plays to be presented.

> The plays proposed to be acted are of a more literary nature than are usually acted in theatres, and are not expected to appeal to a popular audience. . . . There are two plays proposed to be acted, namely a play by Mr. W. B. Yeats called *The Countess Cathleen*, and a play by Mr. Edward Martyn called *The Heather Field*, both being exemplifications of Irish life, and copies of the plays, which are published works, can, if desired, be submitted to you or to any person named on behalf of the Council. Also it is possible that there may be a short dialogue in the Irish language.[40]

That accomplished, Yeats and his friends turned their attention to publicizing their venture and to the practical problems of hiring a hall, contracting actors, and conducting rehearsals. During this time, Æ (George W. Russell) wrote to Martyn, giving an imaginative suggestion for set design. Although he claimed to 'know nothing about stage mechanism', he proposed:

> The scene painting must be a large item in the expense of production. . . . Would it not be possible to get over this difficulty by the use of coloured photos of scenery, the castles at Gort, etc. used as magic lantern slides and flung from behind a thin hanging? It would be infinitely more illusive in its effect than any painting. The same could be done for most of the scenes in Yeats's *Countess Cathleen*. In fact the idea seems so simple that I imagine it must have been used already. I think it would be worth while thinking it over anyhow. If not capable of use just now, the idea may be of value at another time. It would be also very easy to change one scene to another. If you thought it worth while to ascertain the pos-

26

sibility of this, I imagine it would be well to write to some of the popular entertainers who use limelight views or the instrument makers. They would know to what extent the views could be enlarged.[41]

It was apparently about this time that Yeats and Martyn first discussed the project with George Moore, a close friend of Martyn and an expatriate Irish landlord, who was now widely touted as 'the English Zola' for his excellent realistic novels such as *Esther Waters*. In his droll three-volume reminiscence, *Hail and Farewell*, Moore gives probably only a semi-accurate account of this meeting and of the subsequent ineptitudes of Yeats, Martyn and Florence Farr at rehearsal. The entire tone of this section of *Hail and Farewell* is wittily condescending, and describes how the expert, Moore, takes pity on the follies of the feckless amateurs.

It is true that Moore did have some practical experience of the stage. He was a frequent tilter at the London critics and had early advocated the establishment in London of an equivalent of Antoine's Théâtre Libre. He was on the committee of J. T. Grein's Independent Theatre, an historic group which, whatever its artistic shortcomings, did champion Ibsen and did give to Bernard Shaw his first production. In response to a challenge by a popular boulevard dramatist, G. R. Sims, Moore polished up an earlier rejected play, *The Strike at Arlingford*, and it was presented by the Independent Theatre on 21 February 1893. One typical contemporary review remarked, 'With much to be commended in Mr. Moore's play, there is much to be deplored.' What was to be deplored was that:

. . . the central theme is tamely handled. There is no fight between the women — typical of Capital and Labour — for the omnipotent Reid. Lady Anne gets him for the asking. The momentous nature of the struggle was never felt. The scent of the strikers was never got over the footlights. The play did not palpitate as it should with the passions of the starving miners. Reid reflected nothing but himself. Lady Anne seemed fighting for no stake in particular. Worst of all, the people expressed themselves in language over which lay the trail of the literary man. Nothing destroys the sense of reality like high falutin' phrases, and in *The Strike* Mr. Moore's heroine being a little

27

upset is "distraught", his hero's thoughts "throng his brain in giddy exultation", and so on — the result being that half the house comes to the conclusion that not one of the characters, save the Baron, has anything in his veins but midnight oil and ink.[42]

J. T. Grein himself thought that the play was a *succès d'estime* which failed largely because the leading actors were inadequate. The result, he wrote years later, was 'totally unmagnetic'.[43] Actually, although the review quoted above is generally just in its disparagements, the language was less stiff than Moore's later *The Bending of the Bough*. And although the play is now dated, and was even in 1893 a far cry from Ibsen or Shaw, it was better than, say, Henry James' attempts at dramatic writing. One might conclude that, while Moore did have a greater knowledge of the stage than either Yeats or Martyn, he was far from being the maestro that *Hail and Farewell* suggests.

*   *   *

Florence Farr, who began the rehearsals, was an amateur actress who had the distinction of having love affairs with both G. B. Shaw and W. B. Yeats. 'She attached,' Shaw remarked, 'no more importance to what you call love affairs than Casanova or Frank Harris; and she was too good-natured to refuse anything to anyone she really liked.' The daughter of a well-known sanitary reformer, she was in many ways an English prototype of the New Woman, and she was potentially a fine actress. She made a great impression in an early production of Ibsen's *Rosmersholm*, and she was the original Blanche Sartorius of Shaw's *Widowers' Houses*. With backing from Miss Horniman, as has been mentioned, she produced for the first time, in 1894, Yeats's *The Land of Heart's Desire*, Shaw's *Arms and the Man*, and Todhunter's *A Comedy of Sighs*. Her involvement with Yeats in the Irish Literary Theatre led to her chanting poetry to the accompaniment of the psaltery as an illustration of Yeats's theories of poetic speaking. Yeats regarded her as 'an almost perfect poetic actress' who possessed a beautiful voice. St. John Ervine more caustically remarked that she chanted 'poetry in a rasping manner while she plucked a stringed instrument whose single merit was that it had only one string which was easily broken. This chanting was called 'cantilating', and was a melancholy noise.' Shaw regarded cantilating as nothing at all new:

> Yeats thinks so only because he does not go to church. Half the curates in the kingdom cantilate like mad all the time. Toastmasters cantilate. Public speakers who have nothing to say cantilate. . . . Sarah Bernhardt's abominable "golden voice", which has always made me sick, is cantilation, or, to to use the customary word, intoning. It is no use for Yeats to try to make a distinction: there is no distinction, no novelty, no nothing but nonsense.[44]

According to Shaw, Florence Farr's real difficulty was that she would never exert herself sufficiently to learn her craft. He must probably be considered on these matters a better judge than Yeats, and his letters to Miss Farr are full of exhortation to work at the technique of acting rather than to rely on the inspiration of the moment. He advised her, for instance, to study phonetics under Henry Salt. 'I have never been able to knock enough articulation into you, though you are much better than you were,' he wrote.

> You still think of how you are doing your recitations instead of what you are saying. The final consonant withers, and the light of the meaning goes out every now and then as you attend to your psaltery instead of to your business. At which moments I feel moved to throw things at you. And Yeats is heaping fresh artificialities and irrelevances and distractions and impertinances on you instead of sternly nailing you to the simple point of conveying the meaning and feeling of the author.[45]

The following account by George Moore of the rehearsal of *The Countess Cathleen* seems to make the same point, that Miss Farr was an attractive amateur dazzled by the glamour of art and bored by the labour necessary to achieve it. He and Yeats, he writes:

> . . . sat down together to listen to *The Countess Cathleen*, rehearsed by the lady who had put her psaltery aside and was going about with a reticule on her arm, rummaging in it from time to time for certain memoranda, which when found seemed only to deepen her difficulty. Her stage-management was all right in her notes, Yeats informed me:

"But she can't transfer it from paper to the stage," he said, without appearing in the least to wish that the stage-management of his play should be taken from her. At that moment the voice of the experienced actress [May Whitty] asking the poor lady how she was to get up the stage drew my attention from Yeats to the reticule, which was searched unsuccessfully for a satisfactory answer. The experienced actress walked up the stage and stood there looking contemptuously at Miss Vernon [Moore's name for Miss Farr], who laid herself down on the floor and began speaking through the chinks. Her dramatic intention was so obscure that perforce I had to ask her what it was, and learned from her that she was evoking hell.

"But the audience will think you are trying to catch cockroaches." [46]

*　　*　　*

There were other difficulties than those of casting and rehearsing. Edward Martyn, who had guaranteed the money for the production, began to worry about the orthodoxy of *The Countess Cathleen*, and submitted it to a clerical friend who denounced it. For a time it seemed as if Martyn might withdraw his support, but Yeats submitted the play to two other clergymen and received approving opinions, which helped to calm Martyn's fears. The only person who seemed disappointed by this happy outcome was George Moore, who lost the opportunity to write an essay on Edward Martyn and his Soul. Yeats wrote to Lady Gregory that Moore said, 'It was the best opportunity I ever had. What a sensation it would have made! Nobody has ever written that way about his most intimate friend. What a chance! It would have been heard of everywhere.' [47]

Reading *The Countess Cathleen* today, one finds it difficult to understand its controversial nature. However, the reasons for the opposition to the play were basically the same as those impelling the better-known later controversies surrounding Synge's *The Playboy of the Western World* and O'Casey's *The Plough and the Stars*. The reasons are probably three. Ireland was, and to some extent still is, in the grip of a hyper-sensitive, hyper-puritanical public morality, that was quick to sense slights, whether intentional or not and whether blatant or obscure, against religion and a rather narrow morality. Second, this tender moral sensitivity was paralleled by a patriotic sensitivity that was just as quick to take offence, and whose tenderness had no doubt been exacerbated by the political futilities since the Parnell split. Third, there was an element of strictly personal rancour, which in this case was directed against Yeats by an old political opponent, F. Hugh O'Donnell, who had been expelled years earlier from the Irish Party by Parnell. Yeats's biographer, Hone, describes O'Donnell as 'a very clever man but half mad from vanity, long political contention and the strain of impecuniosity.' [48]

O'Donnell published a vindictive attack against the play in *The Freeman's Journal*, and when a second letter on the subject was refused publication he published both letters together in a pamphlet called *Souls for Gold*. The pamphlet was distributed in letter-boxes all over Dublin, and the journalistic outcry became so strident that Cardinal Logue, the Primate of Ireland, wrote a letter to the press stating that if Yeats's play was as O'Donnell had represented it no Catholic should attend a performance. The recently re-assured Edward Martyn for once behaved unpredictably and was not influenced by the cardinal's statement, for the cardinal admitted in his letter that he had not read the play.

O'Donnell's pamphlet is frequently referred to but seldom quoted, and indeed it is not worth quoting in full. However, some few excerpts will serve to indicate the nature and tone of the attack:

> In this "Celtic drama" I saw at once many reasons why it continues to lie unrepresented, but not a single reason why it should be called Celtic. . . .
> Out of all the mass of our national traditions it is precisely the baseness which is utterly alien to all our national traditions, the barter of Faith for Gold, which Mr. W. B. Yeats selects as the fundamental idea of his Celtic drama! . . .
> I shall cite but two specimens out of this "Celtic Drama" at present, the one where Celtic peasant, Shemus Rhua, kicks the shrine of the Blessed Virgin to pieces, and the one where the Demon, disguised as an Irish pig, hunts down and slays "Father John the Priest" while reading his breviary, and sticks his soul into his black bag. I crave the pardon of my readers, Catholic or Protestant, for offending their sight with such grotesque impiety. . . .
> Good old Father John, in spite of his prayers and his

31

breviary, killed by the devil in the shape of a brown pig! How Irish! How exquisitely Celtic!

In another scene Mr. W. B. Yeats introduces a Celtic peasant woman who is false to her marriage vows. How very Irish that is too. In another scene there are a pair of Celtic peasants who are thieves, and particularly mean thieves. Is that Irish likewise? . . . Mr. W. B. Yeats seems to see nothing in the Ireland of old days but an unmanly, an impious and renegade people, crouched in degraded awe before demons, and goblins, and sprites, and sowlths, and thivishes, — just like a sordid tribe of black devil-worshippers and fetish-worshippers on the Congo or the Niger. . . .

He has no right to outrage reason and conscience alike by bringing his degraded idiots to receive the kiss of the Mother of God. . . .

Mr. W. B. Yeats is a literary artist. He has found for his English readers what is described as a new vein of literary emotion. The transfusion of what is alleged to be the spirit of the Celtic past into modern English is hailed as quite an agreeable diversification of the Stage Irishman dear to the London caricaturist. Instead of Donnybrook and Ballyhooley, or rather by the side of these types, and, as it were, suggesting their development, the genial Anglo-Saxon is asked to regard the fine old Celtic peasant of Ireland's Golden Age, sunk in animal savagery, destitute of animal courage, mixing up in loathsome promiscuity the holiest name of the Christian Sanctuary with the gibbering ghoul-and-fetish worship of a Congo negro, selling his soul for a bellyful, yelling alternate invocations to the Prince of Darkness and the Virgin Mary. Surely this is a dainty dish to set before our sister England. . . .

What hideous silliness, and what hideous profanity! . . . But the utter idiotcy [sic] of it all puts even the impiety in the shade. I will not ask if Mr. W. B. Yeats has any sense of reverence. But has he any good taste, any sense of the becoming and the decent? . . . What is the meaning of this rubbish? How is it to help the national cause? How is it to help any cause at all? . . . There is no reason for tolerating the preposterous absurdity . . . which would degrade Ancient Ireland into this sort of witch's cavern of ghouls and vampires, and abject men and women, and blaspheming shapes from hell. . . .[49]

This was silly, but the bluster, the repetitions, and the judicious selection of certain passages out of context all helped to incite an hysterical reaction, that made the opening of the Irish Literary Theatre seem at the time dangerous and problematical.

*　　*　　*

Nevertheless, the project was publicly launched in early January by a letter from Yeats, which was published in *The Freeman's Journal*.[50] In it, he remarked that he and some friends had hoped a year or so earlier to found an Irish Literary Theatre, 'to do for Irish dramatic literature . . . what the Théâtre Libre and the Théâtre de L'Oeuvre have done for French dramatic literature.' He recounted their hopes to take a theatre or hall for a few days each spring, and also the difficulties they had had in getting the law changed so that they would be able to perform. Now the law had been changed, and so in May two plays would be presented — Martyn's *The Heather Field* and his own *The Countess Cathleen*. He also mentioned that Standish O'Grady, George Moore, and Miss Fiona MacLeod[51] had become interested in writing plays for the theatre in subsequent years. Finally, he listed the names of some of the more impressive guarantors for the theatre, and remarked that the National Literary Society was also assisting with the project.

On 16 January there was a meeting of the National Literary Society, and the following is an extract from the Minutes:

> Mr. W. B. Yeats and Mr. Edward Martyn being in attendance, by arrangement, the project of an "Irish Literary Theatre" was discussed. Mr. Yeats stated that he wished the project developed and carried out under the auspices of the National Literary Society. After a long discussion the following three resolutions were drafted: —
>
> I.   "That this Council do hereby appoint a Sub-Committee to be called 'The Irish Literary Theatre Committee' consisting of Dr. George Sigerson, F.R.U.I., W. A. Henderson, W. B. Yeats, Edward Martyn, D.L., and Mrs. George Coffey."
>
> II. "That said Committee have power to co-opt additional members, and to take all steps in furtherance of the project of

33

'The Irish Literary Theatre' provided that they shall not subject the Council to any liabilities without first obtaining the express sanction of this Council by resolution."

III. "That in the event of any surplus of receipts over expenditure accruing from the performances, the amount shall be retained by the National Literary Society, and reserved for the promotion of the objects of the Irish Literary Theatre."

Mr. Joseph Holloway moved and Miss Edith Oldham seconded the adoption separately of these resolutions, which were passed unanimously.

Mr. Martyn voluntarily handed in the following guarantee to be inserted in the Minutes.

"To the President and Council of the National Literary Society. Gentlemen,

"I hereby undertake to hold you harmless and free from any financial liability in connection with the promotion of the Irish Literary Theatre.

(Signed) EDWARD MARTYN." [52]

Another method of arousing interest in the performances was the publication in May of the magazine *Beltaine*, edited by Yeats. It contained a list of the guarantors for the performances; Lionel Johnson's Prologue to *The Countess Cathleen*, which was spoken on the evening of production by Dorothy Paget; Johnson's short essay on the play; George Moore's introduction to *The Heather Field*, reprinted from the published book; a factual account of the rise of Ibsen and Bjornson by C. H. Herford, reprinted from *The Daily Express*; and an article entitled 'The Theatre' by Yeats, which was reprinted from *The Dome*, and later included in *Ideas of Good and Evil*; and a group of unreprinted paragraphs on various topics by Yeats, gathered under the title of "Plans and Methods". After a brief mention of the contemporary drama of Norway and the efforts of the Théâtre Libre in Paris and the Independent Theatre in London, Yeats continued:

The Irish Literary Theatre will attempt to do in Dublin something of what has been done in London and Paris; and, if it has even a small welcome, it will produce, somewhere about the old festival of Beltaine, at the beginning of every spring,

34

a play founded upon an Irish subject. The plays will differ from those produced by associations of men of letters in London and in Paris, because times have changed, and because the intellect of Ireland is romantic and spiritual rather than scientific and analytical, but they will have as little of a commercial ambition. Their writers will appeal to that limited public which gives understanding, and not to that unlimited public which gives wealth; and if they interest those among their audience who keep in their memories the songs of Callanan and Walsh, or old Irish legends, or who love the good books of any country, they will not mind greatly if others are bored.[53]

Then, after mentioning that the Committee of the theatre was considering a production of Denis Florence MacCarthy's translation of Calderon's *St. Patrick's Purgatory* for 1900, and that Fiona Macleod, Standish O'Grady and others had promised plays, he briefly discussed the style of acting and speech in the two plays about to be produced:

In a play like Mr. Martyn's, where everything is subordinate to the central idea, and the dialogues as much like the dialogues of daily life as possible, the slightest exaggeration of detail, or effort to make points where points were not intended, becomes an insincerity. An endeavour has therefore been made to have it acted as simply and quietly as possible. The chief endeavour with Mr. Yeats's play has been to get it spoken with some sense of rhythm.

*   *   *

The two lyrics, which we print on a later page, are not sung, but spoken, or rather chanted, to music, as the old poems were probably chanted by bards and rhapsodists. Even when the words of a song, sung in the ordinary way, are heard at all, their own proper rhythm and emphasis are lost, or partly lost, in the rhythm and emphasis of the music. A lyric meaning, and its rhythm so become indissoluble in the memory. The speaking of words, whether to music or not, is, however, so

35

perfectly among the lost arts that it will take a long time before
our actors, no matter how willing, will be able to forget the
ordinary methods of the stage or to perfect a new method.

*   *   *

Mr. Johnson, in the interpretative argument which he has
written for *The Countess Cathleen*, places the events it describes in the sixteenth century. So Mr. Yeats originally wrote,
but he has since written that he tried to suggest throughout the
play that period, made out of many periods, in which the
events in the folk-tales have happened. The play is not historic, but symbolic, and has as little to do with any definite
place and time as an *auto* by Calderon. One should look for
the Countess Cathleen and the peasants and the demons not
in history, but, as Mr. Johnson has done, in one's own heart;
and such costumes and scenery have been selected as will
preserve the indefinite.[54]

As the May performances approached, the excitement of those
involved in the production increased. James H. Cousins recalled
an amusing encounter with Moore just days before the opening
performance:

Prior to the unique event, which everyone knew was going
to make history, a send-off was given in a reception at which
all the brainy world was present, and some of the possibilities,
including myself. Before the speeches there was an informal
movement in which everybody met everybody else. I noticed
a quaint figure of a man dawdling about passing a remark to
this one and that. He struck me as particular, though I could
not say why. He was notably well-dressed, carried himself with
ease, but his pasty face and vague eyes, and particularly his
straw-coloured hair that looked as if it had been pitchforked
on for the occasion, seemed a contradiction to his air of
distinction. I asked an acquaintance who the comedian was,
and learned that he was George Moore, the novelist who was
more famous than some people thought he ought to be. A few
minutes later I was making some notes in a pocket book
relative to the occasion. To my surprise the novelist came over

36

to me and remarked on the importance of the occasion. "Only a great poet," he said, "would have brought me from London." The reference, I knew, was to Yeats, and I warmed to the novelist for his generosity to a poet. I pondered the phenomenon of so famous a person wasting an opinion on me — and then had a nasty glimmer of an idea that he had mistaken me for a pressman.[55]

Some newspapers saw the new theatre group's potential for offering an alternative to the imported plays then filling the stages. On the Saturday preceding the opening performance, *The Daily Express*, which criticized Yeats's play as un-Irish, nevertheless welcomed the coming productions:

> The Irish Literary Theatre is making a bold effort at reform in a direction where reform is absolutely necessary, and where, if it can be effected, its results will make for immediate and incalculable good. We do not suppose that there was ever any period when the theatre was a greater national influence than it is today in Great Britain and Ireland, or when that influence was more widely perverted and abused. The evil shows itself in a thousand ways, but may always be traced to one cause — the cause which the Irish Literary Theatre seeks to eliminate by the encouragement of an example which has every moral and spiritual claim upon success. Just two hundred years ago Dr. Jeremy Collier published his scathing attack upon the "Immorality and Profaneness of the English Stage", and under that just condemnation the greatest of an age of great playwrights blushed and were silent. Today the same immorality and profaneness — in shapes just as brutal and far more insidious — are flaunted before the eyes and minds of a dramatic public which has a hundred votaries for every one that laughed at *The Country Wife*, or *The Beaux' Stratagem*. And yet the plays at which Collier launched his indignant satire were at least redeemed by the wit and learning of Congreve and Wycherley and Farquhar. The theatre of today has not even this scant excuse to offer for its universal degradation and immorality. Those who are responsible for the production of our modern plays have to make their appeal to a public which a continuous process of vulgarisation has re-

duced to such a level that it no longer required that its vicious pabulum should be dressed with the sauce of intellect or wit. . . . That *The Countess Cathleen* and *The Heather Field* strike an Irish note and aim at a national idea gives them an intimate claim upon Irish support, but their first claim is that they appeal to the intellect and the spirit, and forsake the old familiar appeal to the senses. Whether they be successful acting plays or not is a question which will be decided next week. Whatever way that question be decided it does not affect the purpose of a movement whose object is to furnish an opportunity of submitting to the test of actual performance, year after year, plays which in the present state of public taste, commercial managers could not afford to put on the stage. It is the duty, as we hope it will be the pleasure, of every Irishman to encourage and promote by every means in his power a movement so necessary, so practical, and in its essence so consonant with the best interests of morality and education.[56]

But on the same day, *The Daily Nation*, which was to lead the attack on *The Countess Cathleen*, printed the following leading article:

As may have been seen by a reference to our advertising columns, *The Countess Cathleen*, an "Irish Literary Drama", by Mr. W. B. Yeats, is to be performed, for the first time, in Dublin, on Monday next, the 8th of May. We accepted the advertisement in ignorance of the nature of the drama. Now that we have read it, we wish to protest in the names of morality and religion, and Irish nationality, against its performance. And we hope very earnestly that . . . those Irish Catholics, who may form a portion of the audience, will so give expression to their disapproval as to effectually discourage any further ventures of a similar kind. . . .

The production of such a play as *The Countess Cathleen*, on the occasion of the inauguration of what was intended to be a distinctively national institution, is nothing short of an outrage. The absolute contempt which has been displayed by the promoters and managers of the Irish Literary Theatre for the discrimination, good taste, and self-respect of the citizens of Dublin, is insulting to the last degree. . . . We trust, as we have already said, that those who are responsible for a gross and scandalous breach of faith with the public of this country, will receive their deserts on Monday night in the practical evidence afforded them that the people of the Catholic capital of Catholic Ireland cannot be subjected to affront with impunity.[57]

Quite clearly, this was incitement to riot.

On Monday, 8 May, at the Antient Concert Rooms, the Irish Literary Theatre gave its first performance of Yeats's *The Countess Cathleen*.[58] No matter how destructive the advance comments had been, they served as free publicity for the performances. As James Cousins recalled,

> The coming performances suddenly became a matter of burning national interest; not, however, because of a realisation of the significance of the birth of Irish drama, but because an Irish critic resident outside Ireland had discovered that an incident in *Countess Cathleen* was "an outrage on Catholic sentiment". The Irish Cardinal banned the play without reading it. Charges in the press and replies by the author did what dignified advertising could not do: the house was filled with partizans of both the critics and the author. The offending incident (a famine-demented peasant in a past era kicking a holy shrine to pieces in revulsion against "God and the Mother of God") had been deleted, but it carried a wake of waves in the text, and as each of these appeared, it was received with a storm of hisses by a group of young men who had been instructed by a morning paper to chase the play off the stage. But an answer to the protests broke from another group of young men who, from the point of view of literature or drama would hardly have noticed the hissed lines, but who began to see in them some hidden excellence that stimulated loud applause. In the duel of hiss and cheer, cheer won. I can give my word as to the victory, for I was one of the victors, and possessed as spoils of conquest a hat with a broken rim through which I had clenched my fingers when waving it in wild applause at nothing in the play but something in the rising spirit of the Arts in Ireland as against the spirit of obscurantism and dishonest censorship. From the point of view of publicity the occasion was a howling success.[59]

Joseph Holloway who was, of course, present noted an 'organised claque of about twenty brainless, beardless, idiotic-looking youths [who] did all they knew to interfere with the progress of the play by their meaningless automatic hissing and senseless comments.... Their 'poor spite' was completely frustrated by enthusiastic applause which drowned their empty-headed expressions of dissension.' [60] Seumas O'Sullivan was also there, and years later wrote:

> I was, by chance, in the gallery, and at the fall of the curtain a storm of booing and hissing broke out around the seats in which I and a few enthusiasts were attempting to express our appreciation of the magnificent performance. (I can never forget the exquisite playing and speaking of Florence Farr, who played the part of Aileel, the bard.) But close to me, at the time unknown to me, was a lad who vigorously contributed his share to the applause. It was James Joyce.[61]

T. W. Rolleston in a defence of the demonstration wrote:

> It happens that I was sitting close to the "dozen disorderly boys".... It appeared to me that their expressions of disapproval were not exactly "disorderly".... They expressed their sentiments with vigour, but in a perfectly gentlemanlike manner. They flung no insults at the author or the company; they made no attempt to seriously interfere with the performance, and they applauded as vigorously as anyone, nay, they even led the applause at some of the fine and touching passages in the play.... The impression left on my mind by the whole affair was that a representative Dublin audience had splendidly vindicated, in the teeth of bitter prejudice and hostility, an author's right to a fair hearing for his work, and also that the hostile element in the audience had expressed itself in a manner, which, if one is permitted to be hostile at all, had no trace of malice or stupid violence.[62]

On 9 May *The Freeman's Journal* gave an approving if sententious summation:

> *The Countess Cathleen* has been subjected to a good deal of criticism on moral grounds because of the sentiments to which

40

the evil characters give expression, as if the bad could be otherwise than evil. But there is no confusion of the moral standards in the play, no calling of bad good and of good bad, as has been recently the fashion in several really demoralising plays produced in Dublin. In reality it is a spirit-drama of the "Faust" type, but with a motive far removed from the essentially sensual motive of that much played theme. The presentation of such a play under the conditions described must, of course, make even a greater innovation on the ordinary playgoer's expectations and make success all the more difficult. Themes of the kind have hitherto been presented to the accompaniment of trembling harmonies and Wagnerian discords. To present them in their literary simplicity is to travel very far indeed from the theatrical conventions of the hour. Under the circumstances the promoters of the Irish Literary Theatre must have had their expectations fulfilled last evening. An audience of between four and five hundred assembled to witness the first production of *The Countess Cathleen*. A small knot of less than a dozen disorderly boys, who evidently mistook the whole moral significance of the play, cast ridicule upon themselves by hissing the demons under the impression that they were hissing the poet. But the audience, representative of every section of educated opinion in Dublin, was most enthusiastic, recalling the actors and the author again and again and cheering loudly.[63]

But *The Daily Express* found less to applaud in the play. This hissing was directed against expressions which were 'not, in our opinion, entirely above criticism from certain points of view'. Indeed, not only were the protests defensible, but Yeats's play itself was not dramatically effective — a criticism, incidentally, to be levelled at many of Yeats's plays in the ensuing years.

From the passages we have quoted its great poetic beauty will be seen, but poetic beauty is not the same as dramatic beauty, and we think it can hardly be denied that the problem of presenting an action on the stage in which the sequence of events shall at once satisfy the intellect as being natural and inevitable, and satisfy the imagination as forming an artistic

41

harmony, has not been fully solved. The demons have in them too much or too little power over material things; the Countess is ready to give up her soul for her people, but she never goes to the hut, close to her door, when they are thronging to sell, to entreat them to be mindful of their eternal weal. The personages and events are no doubt intended to be placed in an unreal mystical world, but they pass over the borderland now and then, and are either not real enough or not unreal enough to be fully accepted by the reader's imagination. Defects of this kind will occur to every reader and indicate a certain want of expression in dramatic composition — by far the hardest and also the noblest form of poetry — which will probably be largely remedied in Mr. Yeats's future work. We venture to think, however, as regards that work, that Mr. Yeats would do well to leave the presentation of the Irish peasantry and their religious atmosphere to those who know them intimately. Mr. Yeats is a king in fairyland — in the world of imaginative symbol and spiritual thought — but he does not know the Irish peasant and what he believes and feels, and the Irish peasantry in this play are, and always were, totally incapable of the acts and sayings attributed to them. We do not say that they are too good or too wise or too religious, but merely that their minds are not made that way. The conception that "God and the Mother of God have dropped asleep" or the central conception of the excessive value of a beautiful Countess's soul . . . are ideals absolutely foreign to anything that can be called Irish in character and spiritual outlook. That genuine dramatic faculty is shown in the play is undeniable, but to write a perfectly satisfactory stage drama Mr. Yeats needs training, experience, and knowledge of humanity in the concrete.[64]

The acting, particularly of May Whitty and of Florence Farr, was much admired, but no commentator gives a vivid or even particularly clear impression of how the actors looked, how they sounded, how they moved, or what they did. Apparently the production was not exactly a smoothly professional one, and its defects may have been somewhat glossed over in the generally enthusiastic response which the occasion evoked. Holloway, at any rate, did remark:

Much of the last act was spoiled by a creaky door, and the too liberal use of palpable tin-tray-created thunder claps. The staging was good if unpretentious, and the dresses excellent; and the piece went without a hitch, although the stage room was somewhat scanty.[65]

However, the honest lowbrow from *The Evening Herald* remarked, 'Indeed, the whole performance was weird.'

On 10 May *The Daily Nation* printed the following letter which it had solicited from Cardinal Logue:

Dear Sir — You invite my opinion on the play of Mr. Yeats, *The Countess Cathleen*. All I know of the play is what I could gather from the extracts in Mr. O'Donnell's pamphlet and your paper. Judging by these extracts, I have no hesitation in saying that an Irish Catholic audience which could patiently sit out such a play must have sadly degenerated, both in religion and patriotism.

As to the opinions said to have been given by Catholic divines, no doubt the authors of these opinions will undertake to justify them; but I should not like the task if it were mine.— I am, dear sir, yours faithfully,

MICHAEL CARDINAL LOGUE[66]

On 11 May the *Independent* printed an outspoken letter from Frederick Ryan, who was in years to come to be an actor, writer and secretary for the Irish National Theatre Society.

Sir — In view of the "set" which is being made in some quarters on Mr. W. B. Yeats's play, *The Countess Cathleen*, and the unblushing appeals to religious bigotry and intolerance which it has occasioned, it is necessary, I think, for those who still value mental freedom, to protest against the monstrous claim that is thereby set up. With Mr. Yeats's verse or Mr. Yeats's philosophy I am not now concerned. The thesis of his play may be approved or disapproved. But everyone who values intellectual liberty is concerned to claim for Mr. Yeats his right to express his thought. On that ground — whilst one can quite understand Mr. Yeats's difficulties — it is, I think, to be regretted that he should have adopted the line of defence

43

he did on Saturday. It is surely somewhat humiliating that a fine poet, as Mr. Yeats undoubtedly is, who sets himself to a serious and intellectual task, should feel obliged to go, cap in hand, as it were, to "two Catholic divines" before presenting his work to an audience of his countrymen. Let us get out of this stifling atmosphere of restriction and petty, insincere bigotry. Let us claim for Mr. Yeats — if he will not claim it for himself — his full right, in common with every other man's, to the free expression of his thought, even if fifty newspaper theologians denounced him, or a hundred "Catholic divines" howled their anathemas. The Irish Literary Theatre, and the movement with which it is connected, claims to foster intellectual life in Ireland. I would remark that this object would be better attained by taking the boldest and most impregnable position, than by pandering to, or even countenancing the ignorant prejudices of the least enlightened of our people. Surely, we have not got to the stage yet of bowing down before *The Daily Nation*, or taking our views from a prelate whose conception of public conduct is such as to enable him to denounce a work he has not read, on the strength of some distorted extracts. — Yours, etc.,

FREDERICK RYAN[67]

On 12 May the readers of *The Daily Nation* heard again from O'Donnell:

Dear Sir — There can be no doubt about it, there are two versions of the repulsive *Countess Cathleen*. Only in the one for his London public does Mr. W. B. Yeats set his new model Celtic peasant "to kick to pieces" the shrine of the Blessed Virgin. In the version for his Dublin admirers "the young bard" of West Britain has remembered that prudence is a virtue. But we are now entitled to inquire will Mr. W. B. Yeats place his London public also in possession of his cautious resolution? Though small, it should not be deceived by the fond imagination that W. B. Yeats achieved with impunity the glory of Cromwell.

I have also failed to perceive, even in the gurgling gush of the "Dull'un's Journal" and the "Rhodesian Dependent" that another Yeatsite showpiece, "The Slaying of Father John by the Demon Swine", has been preserved to point the way to those moral and intellectual ideals which the Rhodesians tell us are yet in store for Papist Dublin.

I think that there is one matter, however, which can fully console all who strove to dyke back the flood of mawkish nastiness which was being let loose upon the country, and this is the high-minded witness to Irish honour and Irish Faith which, in noble contradistinction to a couple of Catholic reptile journals, was borne by such Protestant organs as *The Daily Express* and *The Irish Times*.

The Daily Express's rebuke of Mr. W. B. Yeats's anti-Irish blasphemies is none the less crushing because it strives to spare the silly offender. . . .

The Irish Times, while stating the dismal "failure" of the miserable "drama", takes occasion, in reference to Mr. W. B. Yeats's "ideal" of Souls for Gold, to declare with generous pride that the barter of spiritual life for physical advantage is simply abhorrent to "the history of Ireland" and of the entire "Celtic Nation".

Hurrah for the Irish Protestant who remains an Irishman!— I remain, dear sir, yours faithfully,

F. HUGH O'DONNELL[68]

And on 10 May a group of students at the Royal University in Dublin, not including James Joyce, submitted a letter to the editors of various newspapers protesting the performances of *The Countess Cathleen*. It concludes, 'we feel it our duty, in the name and for the honour of Dublin Catholic students of the Royal University, to protest against an art, even a dispassionate art, which offers as a type of our people a loathsome brood of apostates.' [69]

In general, however, the production was regarded as a vindication of Yeats and of the effort, and the production of Martyn's less esoteric *Heather Field* on the following evening was quite unmarred by hissing from the gallery. *The Freeman's Journal* reported:

The success which attended the experiment of establishing an Irish Literary Theatre when its inaugural play, *The Countess Cathleen* was produced on Monday, developed last night into something very nearly approaching a triumph when Mr. Edward Martyn's drama, *The Heather Field*, was put on the

45

boards. The audience was again a distinguished one, but not so large as on the previous occasion. On the other hand, however, there was no hostile element present, a circumstance which gave Mr. Martyn's play a great advantage over Mr. Yeats's, and allowed the story to be followed without interruption from the gradual awakening of interest in it to its tragic and beautiful conclusion. . . . Here . . . is a play that reveals a tragedy of social and domestic life although there is not the remotest suggestion in it from beginning to end of the disordered eroticism which is responsible for so many stage successes in London and Paris during recent years. . . .

No description of this moving and beautiful play can possibly convey any idea of its pathos and power. The drama reads well, but it plays superbly. And it was acted last night with a finish and completeness which no one could have looked for on so limited a stage. The Carden Tyrrell of Mr. Thomas Kingston was an interpretation which satisfied the artistic sense fully, and vividly realised the author's conception. . . . Altogether *The Heather Field* was a remarkable success. From first to last it was punctuated by the warmest applause, and at the end its author was called before the curtain and received with loud and long-continued cheering.[70]

The Evening Herald called the play 'A fine wholesome drama', while the *Independent* gushed that, 'It is impossible to speak in moderation of Mr. Edward Martyn's drama, *The Heather Field*, which was produced by the Irish Literary Theatre last night. The power, the beauty, and the excellence of Mr. Martyn's work took everyone by storm. . . .' *The Irish Times*, however, came closer to the evaluation which the play would probably receive today:

Now, so far as the every day play-goer is concerned, *The Heather Field* will scarcely excite anything like the feelings that it would seem to have produced in Mr. Moore; to many it may appeal as a deep analysis of human nature, as an effort to read into life as it exists round about us mystical and exalted readings, but to a man who goes to a play to be amused, instructed, or initiated into the workings of the main-springs of human conduct, *The Heather Field* is little likely to be of any assistance. . . . Apart altogether from that, *The*

Heather Field is wearisome because it has no action worthy of
the name; its dialogue is stilted; its characters are not very
deftly drawn; and its reflection of Irish life is not very convincing. The cold methods of the Norwegian dramatists can
never be applied with any truth to even the Irish landlord . . .
without parodying the very essences of Irish life.[71]

Max Beerbohm, who had succeeded Bernard Shaw as drama critic
of *The Saturday Review*, had attended the performances and also
the congratulatory dinner which *The Daily Express* gave for the
Literary Theatre on 11 May at the Shelbourne. One feels that he
may have been somewhat carried away by the *bonhomie* of the
occasion, for he remarked in his *Saturday Review* notice:

> Not long ago this play was published as a book, with a preface
> by Mr. George Moore, and was more or less vehemently dis-
> paraged by critics. Knowing that it was to be produced later
> in Dublin, and knowing how hard it is to dogmatise about a
> play till one sees it acted, I confined myself to a very mild
> disparagement of it. Now that I have seen it acted, I am sorry
> that I disparaged it at all. It turns out to be a very powerful
> play, indeed. For the benefit of my colleagues, I may add that
> it has achieved a really popular success in Dublin — a success
> which must be almost embarrassing to the founders of a
> Literary Theatre.[72]

When the play, with substantially the Dublin cast, was given one
afternoon performance at Terry's Theatre in London on 6 June,
Beerbohm's colleagues drew the following conclusions:

> The actors were not to blame if *The Heather Field* did not
> altogether please. (*The Echo*)

> Mr. George Moore, having delivered himself of the pronounce-
> ment that Mr. Edward Martyn, the author of *The Heather
> Field*, and Shakespeare are our only two dramatists, there
> remains little for anyone else to add — except that if Mr.
> Martyn is in need of an armorial motto, he might choose "Save
> me from my friends." (*The Daily Mail*)

47

... a drama of drainage, wandering wearily around the question of agricultural improvements and the relations of a dreaming and insane Irish proprietor with his tenants and the Land Commission can have no chance of popular success. (*The Daily Telegraph*)

... it says a great deal for the acting that *The Heather Field* is endurable on the stage at all. (*The Times*)

... very dull and gloomy. (*The Standard*)

No; *The Heather Field* may be "literary drama", but is not "acting drama". (*The Daily Mail*)

*   *   *

George Moore did not come over to Dublin for the first nights, and so Martyn, with more flamboyance than usual, telegraphed him, 'The sceptre of intelligence has passed from London to Dublin.' [73] Holloway wrote more prosaically in his journal, 'Beyond a doubt, the admirable performance of *The Heather Field* has made the Irish Literary Theatre an unmistakably established fact, and an institution which all Irish people of culture and refinement ought to be justly proud of.' [74]

To celebrate the success of the project, on 11 May 1899, *The Daily Express* gave a dinner at the Shelbourne Hotel for those involved in the productions. George Moore had arrived in Dublin by then, and attended it, as did Yeats, Martyn, Douglas Hyde, John Eglinton, Max Beerbohm, John O'Leary, Standish O'Grady, and others. The opening speech by T. P. Gill, the newspaper's editor, reflects the cordiality of the occasion; he did not deny his newspaper's opposition to Yeats's play, but nevertheless saw great promise in the venture:

They had had an exciting week in Ireland (hear, hear), a week which would be memorable in the literary history of the country (applause). For the first time Ireland, which, goodness knew, had known plenty of excitement from other causes, had been profoundly stirred upon an intellectual question. He regarded the controversy which Mr. Yeats's play had aroused as one of the best signs of the times (applause). It showed that

48

they had reached at last the end of the intellectual stagnation
of Ireland (hear, hear), and that, so to speak, the grey matter
of Ireland's brain was at last becoming active (hear, hear). . . .
In the Irish Literary Theatre movement they had the support
of men of different views upon many matters, including, he
believed, the theology of "Countess Cathleen" (laughter and
applause). They were not required to surrender their freedom
of judgment in respect to that production or any production
which they hoped would be placed upon the stage from year
to year (applause). For his own part, he was free to say that
while he was a great admirer of Mr. Yeats's poetry and the
wonderful beauty of his *Countess Cathleen*, he . . . did not
regard the play as by any means the best of Mr. Yeats's works,
as there were, no doubt, some who did, and he would not
accept it as a presentation of the life and character of Ireland,
if it were offered to them as such (applause). The thoughts of
those cowering hinds did not represent the attitude of the Irish
peasantry towards the things of their religion (applause). Might
he say that he claimed that they should treat with respect the
feelings of those who, taking Mr. Yeats's play very literally as
a piece of realism, had expressed the strongest dissent upon
these points (hear, hear). . . . What should he say of Mr.
Martyn? (Applause). He . . . produced a great and original
play, and that Ireland had discovered in him a dramatist fitted
to take rank among the first in Europe (loud applause). . . .
There was now the opportunity for the regular theatrical
managers . . . they might do worse than take *The Heather
Field* with its company just as it stood, and put it for a week
on the stage at the Gaiety or the Royal.

Yeats spoke next, and referred to the controversy raised:

At last, apathy and cynicism, deep besetting sins of their
country, were beginning to evaporate (applause), and, like the
chairman, he welcomed exceedingly the controversy which had
arisen about his play. . . . There were the issues which they
should always be fierce upon, but they were the only issues in
this country which they were accustomed to treat with entire
apathy (applause). His only regret in connection with the whole
matter was that Cardinal Logue, who was such a good friend

49

to national movements like that of the Gaelic League . . .
should have been misled about the nature of the play. However, he . . . hoped that if ever Cardinal Logue ever found
leisure to read the play, he would discover how deeply he had
been misled. He [Yeats] had not singled any particular argument that moved him [Logue] to write that letter. He . . .
must therefore simply summarise very shortly what had been
said against his play and answer it. He did not answer it in the
hope of convincing the most ardent of his opponents. He spoke
"not to convert those who did not believe, but to protect those
who did" (laughter). The chief arguments against the play were
three: first that the story was German, secondly that he had
blasphemed in it, and thirdly that he had slandered the
country. A very ingenious antagonist was anxious to prove that
the play was not Celtic, and therefore looked to a country
which by common consent was not Celtic, and pitched upon
Germany. Well, as a matter of fact, a well-known writer told
them that it was an Irish story, and in Mr. Larminie's book,
West Irish Folk-Tales and Romances, it was, he believed,
stated that the story was one of those imaginative fables which
go through all countries and belong to no country. The argument that he was a blasphemer was a very simple one. The
utterances of the demons and lost souls had been described as
the beliefs of himself (laughter). The charge that he had
slandered the country was worked out with great ingenuity. It
was said Mr. Yeats had made the peasants thieves and the
women false to their husbands, and it was asked is that Celtic?
Well, he was ready to admit that nobody ever robbed in
Ireland, and that no woman ever false to her husband. That
might be true, but it was perfectly irrelevant, for, after all, it
was nothing against the truth of a thing to say that it never
happened (laughter and applause). His play, of course, was
purely symbolic, and as such it must be regarded. Literature
was the expression of universal truths by the medium of
particular symbols; and those who were working at the
National Literary movement and at all such movements were
simply trying to give to universal truths the expression which
would move most the people about them. In all countries
where suffering had made patriotism a passion they had found
literature turning to that patriotism as to its most powerful

re-echo (applause). On that they must rely if they were to stir the people of the country profoundly. This was the great sword that had been put into their hands, and what they had to do was to spiritualise the patriotism and the drama of this country. What time had in store for them the future alone would tell; but it looked as if the writers of this country were seeking for spiritual things and lifting their voice against that externality, that worship of power, and the worship of merely external magnificence which seemed to be spreading over the English-speaking races (applause).

Martyn, Beerbohm and others spoke very briefly, and then George Moore expressed his enthusiasm for the revival he now saw as beginning:

> I feel conscious that I must seem like a man who, having deserted his mother for a long time, returns to her with effusion when he hears that she has become rich and powerful. . . . There have been since the ancient bards, poets of merit, competent poets, poets whom I do not propose you should ever forget or think less of; but Ireland, so it seems to me, has had no poet who compares for a moment with the great poet of whom it is my honour to speak tonight. It is because that I believe that in the author of *The Countess Cathleen*, Ireland has discovered her ancient voice, that I have undertaken this journey from London, and consented to what I have hitherto considered to be the most disagreeable task that could befall me — a public speech. I should not have put myself to the inconvenience of a public speech for anything in the world, except a great poet, that is to say a man of exceptional genius, who was born at a moment of great national energy. This was the advantage of Shakespeare and Victor Hugo as well as Mr. Yeats. The works of Mr. Yeats are not as yet, and probably never will be, as voluminous as those of either the French or English poet, but I cannot admit that they are less perfect. The art of writing a blank verse play is so difficult that none except Shakespeare and Mr. Yeats have succeeded in this form. This assertion will seem extravagant, but think a moment and you will see that it is nearer the truth than you will suppose. We must not be afraid of praising Mr. Yeats's poetry too much;

51

we must not hesitate to say that there are lyrics in the collected poems as beautiful as any in the world. We must be courageous in front of the Philistine and insist that the lyric entitled "Innisfree" is unsurpassable. Had the Irish poets who came before Mr. Yeats had the same advantage as Mr. Yeats, they might have written as well. We will give them the benefit of the doubt, and it is only fair to assume that Mr. Kipling, the poet that England is now celebrating, would not have written the most hideous verses ever written in a beautiful language, if he had not lived in a specially hideous moment.[75]

*   *   *

The attention given by historians to the Irish Literary Theatre has obscured the fact that work was being done quietly in the provinces by other Irishmen, to further the cause of an Irish drama. For instance, the following letter by Alice Milligan[76] was printed in *The Daily Express* on 21 January, and mentions what must be the first modern production in the Irish language:

Sir — Mr. W. B. Yeats, in his interesting letter of Saturday last on the Irish Literary Theatre,[77] made references to the dramatic entertainments given in connection with the recent Aonach Tir-Conail at Letterkenny, Co. Donegal, and quoted the success of those ventures as encouraging him to believe that plays appealing to the higher intelligence of an audience can attain success.

Having taken part in the production of one of these plays, *The Passing of Conall*,[78] I think that I may be permitted to express an opinion on the subject. Opinion when founded on experience, is always of value, and, *en passant*, let me say that I think *The Daily Express*, which is setting a good example to the Press of Ireland in so many things, might very well set the example in refusing to publish correspondence such as that in Wednesday's paper, over the signature, "A West Briton", on the subject of learning Irish. When an opinion is expressed by a person whose ignorance is palpable, why should it be inflicted on the intelligent reading public in the shape of a letter

52

to the Press? A "West Briton's" assertion that Irish language and literature are extinct is as untrue as that the world is flat, or that two and two make five, and *The Express* editor, knowing this well, might very well act as dictator.

This is apparently a digression from the main subject of my letter, but is not so in fact. Both Mr. Yeates [*sic*], as an Irish literary man, and a "West Briton" will be interested to know that a main feature of the Letterkenny play was the introduction of an act written in Gaelic verse by a living Gaelic poet, and enacted by Gaelic speakers. The experiment was so successful that Dr. Douglas Hyde, Miss Norma Borthwick, and other leading members of the Gaelic League, present at the production, were convinced of the importance of using the stage to promote the revival of the native Irish language as a medium of literature and culture. The next Oireachtas, which will be held in Dublin at the end of May, will likely be the occasion of a dramatic entertainment in which the Irish language alone will be used, and which, at the same time, will be instructive and attractive to those who only understand English and other foreign languages. Ancient Irish legendary literature gives us in the Ossianic dialogues the nearest approach to drama in an ancient native literature. Taking the disputes between Oisin and St. Patrick as a basis, I have sketched for the Gaelic League a dramatic entertainment which has met with approval, though it is not yet formally adopted by any committee.

I have suggested that a few members of the League in Dublin, who have considerable elocutionary power, should impersonate the aged Oisin, Patrick, and his clerics, and that from the old versions of the dialogues some of our poets should condense the most important parts, embodying Oisin's laments for his lost comrades, Fin and the Fianna, a narrative of the elopement of Diarmuid and Grainne, and his own wanderings to Tir-nan-oig. During the narration, Oisin, by magic art, is to summon up for the benefit of the astonished clerics visions of the chief scenes in his heroic youth. These in a series of beautiful tableaux, appearing behind a gauze curtain in an inner stage, will form the chief feature of the entertainment.

In Belfast last May during Feis Ceoil week, we produced such tableaux with undoubted success, our subjects being

53

scenes from the story of Cuchulain and the Flight of Diarmuid and Grainne. In Belfast they were accompanied by an explanatory lecture given by T. O'Neill Russell. A step in advance will be taken in Dublin by introducing a dramatic setting and also by using only the native language.

Our venture will come off most likely a full month after the production of Mr. Yeats's and Mr. Martyn's plays, and the fact that the Gaelic League has theatrical ambitions will only increase public interest in the National Literary Theatre's dramas. We will have much to learn from each other, and perhaps our Gaelic production will lead Mr. Yeats to decide on dramatising or adapting his own Wanderings of Oisin for the Literary Theatre to produce in the first year of the next century.

Very truly,

ALICE L. MILLIGAN[79]

The productions referred to were those given at the Aonach Tir-Conail on 18 November 1898, at Letterkenny, Co. Donegal. During the week's festivities, an operetta, *Finola*, by Brendan J. Rogers and Sister Mary Gertrude, was performed; also presented were two plays on Irish subjects: *The Coming of Conall*, by Sister Mary Gertrude, and acted by students of the Sisters of Loreto Convent, and an anonymous play, possibly by Father Eugene O'Growney, entitled *The Passing of Conall*. The last named was the most important, as it contained one scene in Irish. *The Freeman's Journal* reported on its performance:

> Tonight before a crowded audience the first public performance took place of the Irish drama *The Passing of Conall*. The hero, the ancestor of the Clan O'Donnell, is shown in his old age appealing to Saint Caillin of Fermagh to grant him a vision of the scenes of his youth. The play then proceeds, and there are interesting scenes of Irish life in the fourth and fifth centuries. . . . The drama has been written by a celebrated student of Irish history, and a prominent member of the Gaelic League, who desires to have his identity concealed. . . . One scene, that of St. Patrick at Tara, has been translated into Irish by "Padraic" of the New York Gaelic movement — Mr.

Patrick O'Byrne, now of Killybegs. His translation is very fine and . . . thoroughly preserves the spirit of the original. . . . The scene was acted both in Irish and English.[80]

The scene of St. Patrick at Tara, with its dialogue in Irish, marked the beginning of Gaelic drama. It was presented several times during the next year; in Belfast on 16 March, with P. T. MacGinley and Alice Milligan in the cast, and again on 3 April 1899 in Derry.

The potential for drama in Irish as a means of encouraging the language revival was immediately apparent. Early in 1899, the journal of the language movement, *Fáinne an Lae*, spoke of the need to encourage productions in Irish, and described the types of plays needed:

> While we sympathise with this effort to create an Irish stage, we may be permitted to regret the utter absence of a Gaelic Theatre. If we are not mistaken, this absence has been readily explained by more than one literary wiseacre as due to the lamentable fact that dramatic composition is not in accord with the peculiarities of the Gaelic language Ráiméis! This argument may be classed with those of the great "Celtic" class, which chiefly consist of incantations in which the words "glamour", "mysticism", and "Renaissance" will be found invaluable.
>
> The reason why we have no Gaelic plays is that political troubles made a Gaelic Stage impossible while the literary class still existed, and in later times the disappearance of almost all education from the country prevented any demand for a Gaelic drama from coming into existence. The only attempts that seem ever to have been made in this direction appear in Father O'Carroll's scenes in the early numbers of *The Gaelic Journal* and the sketch produced at the Feis Adhamhnain in Letterkenny last November. The latter should be warmly applauded as an effort to make the Gaelic Drama a reality, and it was a pity that it was not made known more widely. . . . In several of the branches it ought to be possible to produce a little drama. The only real difficulty we can see is that it does not at all follow that the members who have the greatest ability in musical or dramatic work are able to speak Gaelic or that

those who speak Gaelic have any dramatic taste. . . . It is not necessary that such a play should be original, probably it would have to be translated. But it should not be long, for three reasons. First, the difficulty of writing; second, the difficulty of learning and speaking the parts; third and principal, the difficulty of inducing the audience to stand it. But these difficulties would not be as serious in the case of a farce, an historical sketch, or a comedietta. Three, or at most four, characters would be quite enough for such a play, and they should not all be male characters. Melodrama would probably be the safest line of all. Its popularity is perennial, and many a poor play . . . gains greatly by the introduction of a couple of good songs.[81]

The tableaux vivants mentioned above by Miss Milligan relied on delicate and colourful scenes to portray episodes from Irish history and legends. The May 1898 performance in Belfast was the first of these on an Irish subject:

> The Feis Ceoil week ended brilliantly with the unique display of tableaux vivants which came off in the Exhibition Hall on Saturday evening [6 May 1898] under the auspices of the local Gaelic League. For some years back this society had held a sort of Feis Ceoil on its own account, and these concerts have been remarkably successful, but this year, as people might be supposed to be sated with music, the Gaelic League struck out on new lines, and we can heartily congratulate all concerned on the success of their undertaking. . . . The proceedings opened by Dr. St. Clair Boyd introducing as orator and exponent of the first series of tableaux, Mr. O'Neill Russell, the well-known Gaelic scholar and litterateur. Mr. Russell, who has made a special study of the ancient tales of the Red Branch era, explained to the audience that they were about to see representations of real historic persons who flourished in Ireland about the beginning of the Christian era. Maeve, Queen of Connacht, having a grudge against Connor MacNessa of Ulster, invaded the Northern province at the head of her army.
> Her outposts were attacked by a young champion Cuchullin, who met and slew in single combat all the warriors she sent against him. At last she bribed Ferdia, the friend of Cuchullin,

56

a youth, to challenge him to fight. The curtain rising on the first tableau showed Queen Maeve, stately and fair and fierce, in robes of orange and white, listening to the auguries of a dark-haired prophetess, who, with flashing eyes and warning gestures, foretold the dangers of the war in which she was embarking. The second scene showed the Connaught queen enthroned in her tent interviewing her dauntless enemy, the young Ulster champion, a heroic stalwart youth with flowing golden locks, dressed in deerskins, and armed with shield and spear. The queen's daughter, Finnbarr, a young girl, all in white, shrunk in fear and wonder by the side of her beautiful and stately mother. In the next scene Finnbarr was offered as bride to Ferdia, a dark-curled young warrior. Maeve assumed an attitude of entreaty, and had taken from her robe the royal brooch as an additional bribe to the young man to urge him to the combat. Then the curtain rose on the two friends face to face in battle array, but Cuchullin clasps Ferdia's hand and gazed on him in sorrowful reproach. The combat was then represented in several scenes, which were loudly applauded. The champions displayed the most wonderful powers of standing still as statues in strained and difficult attitudes. At length Ferdia was shown dying in his friend's arms bewailed by Queen Maeve, on whom Cuchullin hurled scornful reproaches. . . .

The second series, on Diarmuid and Grainne, was narrated by P. J. O'Shea. The last series was also narrated by him; the subject was Grace O'Malley (Granuaile):

The historical series of tableaux were completed by a series alluding to Grace O'Malley's visit to Queen Elizabeth. The English Queen, in jewelled majesty, sat in state with attendant courtier and lady, and a better Queen Bess could scarcely be imagined. Granuaile, tall, majestic, severely simple, contrasted excellently with her British Majesty, and the red-haired gallowglass who attended her contrasted as markedly with the courtier and lady in ruffs and velvet. The well-known story of Granuaile at Howth was then shown. The child who personified the stolen heir was as good as the best of the grown-up actors, and evidently entered into the spirit of the play as simply as if engaged in a make-believe game in the nursery at home. The ferocious figure of the gallowglass and the enraged Granuaile were most striking. Dark Rosaleen (Ireland) next appeared, amidst rapturous applause, a perfectly beautiful figure, dark-eyed, sad-faced, with a wreath of roses, and harp twined with flowers. This completed the historical series of pictures, and a complete change in the character of the programme re-awakened the curiosity of the audience.[82]

Their popularity as a form of entertainment is testified to by the 1899 performance of tableaux vivants at the Chief Secretary's Lodge in Dublin, based on Yeats's *Countess Cathleen*. Although Yeats had nothing to do with this performance, it was repeatedly brought up in attacks on Yeats in later years, when he was labelled "Dramatic Entertainer for Dublin Castle".[83]

*   *   *

A literary movement was gaining shape rapidly. By the middle of 1899, Yeats could look with confidence to continued growth of the Irish Literary revival. He spoke at a meeting of the College Historical Society, Trinity College, Dublin, to the proposition: 'That any attempt to further an Irish Literary Movement would result in Provincialism.' *The Daily Express* reported:

Mr. Yeats, who was very cordially applauded, in the course of his reply, said that one of the things which had certainly given all of those who worked in this literary movement the greatest possible pleasure, had been the way in which it had been discussed by many different representatives of Irish opinion. They had found an interest taken in the movement which went beyond their expectations, and he hoped the University of Dublin would yet delight to keep watch over all that which was distinctive and racial in this country. He did not believe that a literature rising out of racial characteristics was provincial. A peasant dressed in his national costume was not provincial. The small shopkeeper in the country town dressed in the costume of London or Paris was provincial. Cosmopolitanism had never been a creative power, because cosmopolitanism was a mere mirror in which forms and images reflected themselves. It could not create them, and was the very essence of provincialism. If they went down into any part of England, Ireland, or Scotland, and analysed the things that gave them the impression of provincialism they would find everywhere that they were the cast off fashions, the cast off clothes, the cast off thoughts of some active centre of creative minds. They were, in literature, the opinions which the provincial of Dublin, or of London, or of Edinburgh supposed to be the opinions of London, but which London had cast off many years ago. It was because great cities by their isolation from the tranquil life of the country, and by their great crowds, gradually lost that tranquility in which original ideas grew up, that movements like the Irish literary movement had always been welcomed in centres such as London and Paris. It was a most extraordinary error to suppose, as a speaker, had supposed, that the writers of this movement began it because they had been rejected by critical opinion in England. A charge was indeed made against them by extreme Nationalists that they were a little group of writers forced upon this country by English critics. Only the other day he read in an extreme organ of patriotic opinion, that it was all very well so long as Mr. Yeats wrote for English readers and English critics, "but now that he tried to establish an Irish Literary Theatre it was time to crush him" (laughter). Now that he was bringing into this country cosmopolitan ideas, now was the moment to crush him (renewed laughter). London welcomed the radical ideas of other countries. There came to her from the ends of the world spirits full of lofty thoughts and ideals, just as they came to ancient Rome, and London gradually stifled their creative energy, gradually turned their thoughts into commonplace, gradually ground them in her commercial machine. That was not so in the days when the world was happiest in creative energy. That was not so in Italy or in Greece, and he did not think it would be so in the English-speaking world of the future. It was impossible that those nations which spoke for good or for ill, the English tongue would accept perpetually the ideas of one city, which was no longer moved by any high ideal. America had a national literature, and America wrote in English. Ireland would have a national literature which would be written to a very great extent in English. Scotland would probably again begin to express herself in a way personal to herself, and Australia and South Africa and the other English-speaking countries would sooner or later express their

59

personal life in literature. Henrik Ibsen, who was known to all nations, was once one of the leaders of the National movement in Scandinavian literature. That movement, too, had had its extravagances. There could not be a creation of energy in any country without extravagance. In literature, or politics, or art, or anything else, extravagance was merely the shavings from the carpenter's bench. It was an overflow of energy. It was, no doubt, regrettable; no doubt all human errors were regrettable; but extravagance was far better than that apathy, or cynicism, which were deep-besetting sins here in Dublin. Every Irish writer for many years, every Irish person who had taken up any intellectual Irish question whatever, had found his coldest welcome in his own city. He had sometimes found translators in a foreign land before he had found readers at his own door. Sir Samuel Ferguson lived unknown to what was called the educated opinion of this country. Although he was a most original and distinguished poet, he was unknown in his own city. In taking up the work of giving to Irish intellect a sincere expression of itself they were taking up a work, not for Ireland only, but for the world. Every nation had its word to speak. He believed the work of Ireland was to lift up its voice for spirituality, for ideality, for simplicity in the English speaking world. Ireland had a unique history. But they could not touch upon that. Whatever that history might have been, whatever might be said about it, Ireland would have a destiny shaped by that history. Ireland had prepared herself in sorrow and in self-sacrifice for the destiny which self-sacrifice and sorrow gave always to men and nations. The literature of England at the present day was becoming a glorification of material faith and material wealth. He believed that Ireland with its legends, its profound faith, with its simplicity, with its sincerity, would lift up its voice for an empire of the spirit greater than any material empire. The world was like a great organ. Sometimes the hand of destiny was upon one stop, and sometimes upon another, and as the hand moved along the stops, the nations awoke or slept, spoke or were silent. Yesterday the pre-destined hand rested upon the stop we call Spain. To-day Spain is silent. To-morrow the hand may rest upon the stop that we call Ireland, and Ireland become a part of the music of the world. (Applause).[84]

1900

The main events in 1900 in the commercial theatre were visits by several famous touring companies. In October, Forbes Robertson appeared at the Gaiety in *The Devil's Disciple*, *Othello*, and *Hamlet*. The Gaiety also saw several visits of the D'Oyly Carte Company, while less memorable groups presented the usual crowd-pleasers, such as *San Toy*, *Jim the Penman*, *The Little Minister*, and, of course, *Charley's Aunt*. On 25 August, Mrs. Patrick Campbell played at the Theatre Royal in Maeterlinck's *Pelléas and Mélisande*. Frank Fay, who was still contributing drama reviews to *The United Irishman*, found some fault with the production — there was too much light on the stage, for instance — but he added, 'Mrs. Patrick Campbell was born to play Mélisande; her acting seemed to be flawless. Her tendency to chant, instead of speaking her words, became perfectly charming when the lines to be spoken are those of a poet like M. Maeterlinck.'[1] But a week later, reviewing Mrs. Campbell's production of Rostand's *Les Romanesques*, translated into English as *The Fantasticks*, Fay cited the disgrace of the Dublin audience for laughing at one of the most beautiful speeches in the play. However beautiful the play may have been, the Dublin audience was clearly not yet converted to poetic drama.

*　　*　　*

The provincial audience was treated to nothing quite so esoteric as *Pelléas and Mélisande*. Obscure professional companies, 'fit-up' companies, made the rounds of the 'smalls' in Ireland, presenting what had been, and was to be, their staple fare for years — the tried and true melodrama, the broad comedy, and even the occasional classic. These plays were presented in village halls under the most primitive conditions, and something of this rugged gypsy life may be seen in the reminiscences of Val Vousden:

> I was engaged to play "utility" parts with a dramatic company, which rejoiced in the sub-title of: "The Only Real Company Touring!" . . . I forbear to mention the name of the village where I was going to join this combination. I landed at the little railway station. It was quite dark; it looked as if no

one had been travelling on that train but the engine men, the guard and myself. The lonely porter informed me that the village was about two-and-a-half miles away. There was no possible chance of a lift and therefore there was nothing for it but to 'pad the hoof'.

It was a cold, miserable, October evening of rain. Not ordinary rain. It spat hurtfully in my face. . . .

At last I arrived in the one-street village. There were no street lamps. The only light I could see was the glare from a shop window. To that shop I made my way. . . .

I knocked on the hard counter. No answer. . . . Becoming impatient I kicked the counter. Then a half-ginger, half-grey-haired man with filthy whiskers and a "wounded" spectacles on the end of his nose burst out of a little door at the end of the shop. Waving a newspaper at me he roared:

"I tould ye people afore, there is no lodgin's here, an' I don't know of any lodgin's ayther, an' even if I did, I wouldn't tell ye. So be off to hell outa this or I'll set the bloody dog at ye!"

Well, he recognised I was an actor anyhow! . . .

The drama that evening was *East Lynne*. The Manager asked me if I could manage to study, roughly, the part of Lord Mount Severn. In those days veteran roles were played by the youngsters and the romantic juveniles by toothless old men! However, I managed to pull through despite the fact that I was wearing brown spats over socks and shoes that were not properly dried. The village people thoroughly "enjoyed" themselves, for they wept all through the play.

I recollect a little accident that evening. When Madame Vine threw herself across the dead body of the boy, calling out "Dead! Dead! and never called me mother!" the bed unfortunately collapsed. . . .

I joined another company and reached the proud position of "Star Leading Man". I may not have received a very big salary although I must admit that occasionally it was fabulous — very much so. The scene is laid in Ballystar (let us call it). When we arrived the "Heavyman" — that is the gentleman who played the villain roles — and myself dropped into a tiny public-house near the station. We called for refreshments and were about to enquire about the appreciation of the drama in Ballystar, when the young lady behind the counter became very embarrassed on hearing her mother call out from the kitchen: "Mary! Mary! Take the butther off the counter, the actors have arrived!"

Well, in Ballystar there was only one place in which we could perform, and that was up on a big loft, over stables. I used to dress in one of the stables with the light of a candle stuck on a nail in the wall. There was a horse there, and as he munched his hay he would turn around occasionally to watch me making-up. The animal often became very restless when we were playing a drama that required shots to be fired.

I used to wonder what effect our baritone had on him. In the variety portion of the programme this terrible man would insist on singing. Unfortunately, he was a relation of the Manager's wife; he was the only blot on our fair reputation. Audiences, on the whole, were very patient; but there were some places where they laughed him off the stage. But it was useless. He *would* sing. A few bars from him of *The Heart Bowed Down* would upset the most congenial atmosphere that ever any group of performers could ask for.

He did not confine himself to baritone songs either. I remember one evening in County Galway when he was finishing, in his usual crude manner, the song *When Other Lips*:

> "Then you'll remember,
> You'll remember me!"

a man from the back of the hall shouted: "Yerra, we'll never forget ye!"

It was announced in Ballystar that by special request we would stage Wilson Barrett's famous play, *The Sign of the Cross*, on Thursday evening. We had not played this very popular drama for a long time, as the wardrobe essential for its production had become very shabby. For instance, the white Roman toga I used to wear became so dilapidated that we had to throw it out on the dust-heap. A toga had to be procured by hook or by crook for Marcus Superbus, the Roman Tribune, by Thursday evening.

Now, a toga is not picked up for the asking in a place like Ballystar, and the funds available for new wardrobe were very scarce indeed. Something had to be done. I had a brain-wave. The place where I was lodging was "wondrous neat and clean", especially the bed linen. I had my toga — the white sheets! . . .

I ascended the ladder leading from the stable to the hayloft, where our two-feet-high stage was erected. The loft was packed to suffocation. In the well-known scene when Marcus points to the arena of the lions, "Mercia, come to the light beyond," an unforgettable thing occurred. The "lions" were roaring in the arena, waiting to devour the Christians. I suppose I must give credit where credit is due: our baritone used to do this excellently. Now, whether the *faux pas* was due to my emotional acting or a slight laxity on the part of Nero when he was pinning me up, I do not know. The folds of the toga fell down anyway. . . .

Suddenly there was an outbrust of laughter from the audience which froze me stiff, and my final humiliation came when I discovered that the young lady who was playing Mercia was doubled up with hilarity too! The landlady, you see, was evidently a very economical soul and had converted flour bags into bed linen, so that in full view of the audience was displayed in blue print the trade mark of a well-known Irish flour mill.[2]

*   *   *

An inevitable part of the repertoire of the provincial touring company in Ireland was the patriotic melodrama, such as *The Colleen Bawn* or *The Siege of Limerick*. In its own way, the Irish Literary Theatre also became increasingly patriotic in 1900. Moore and Martyn and even sometimes Yeats discussed the theatre in terms of its relation to the national well-being. In fact, they seemed to be discussing the future of the Irish language, or the pernicious influence of Trinity College, or the imminent Dublin visit of Queen Victoria, more than they were discussing dramatic theories and aesthetic ideals.

This sense of belonging to a great national resurgence was reflected not only in the statements of the theatre's leaders, but also in the generally uncritical enthusiasm with which the plays were received by the press and the public. There was no repetition of a *Countess Cathleen* imbroglio; there was no hint this year of a division between art and patriotism. Indeed, Martyn suggested that English drama was contemptible because England was decadent, and that Irish drama was admirable because Ireland was high-minded and nobly pure. In 1900, there was practically no one to disagree.

In *The Dome* for January, Yeats wrote a high-minded essay on 'The Irish Literary Theatre', in which he speculated that a 'strong imaginative energy' and 'a genius greater than their own' had somehow descended upon the Irish writer. 'Scandinavia,' he wrote, 'is, as it seems, passing from her moments of miracle; and some of us think that Ireland is passing to hers.'[3] In another essay, 'Plans and Methods', which appeared in this year's issue of *Beltaine*, Yeats wrote that Martyn's new play, *Maeve*— and indeed Moore's new play, *The Bending of the Bough*—both symbolised 'Ireland's choice between English materialism and her own natural idealism. . . .'[4] It was a chief function of the theatre 'to bring Ireland from under the ruins' of commercialism and materialism.

George Moore's contribution to *Beltaine* was an article called 'Is the Theatre a Place of Amusement?' In it, he made a distinction between amusement and pleasure:

> People seek amusement, not pleasure, in a theatre. To obtain pleasure in a theatre, a man must rouse himself out of the lethargy of real life; his intelligence must awake, and the power to rouse oneself from the lethargy of real life is becoming rarer in the playgoer and more distasteful to him. . . . The playgoer wants to be amused, not pleased; he wants distraction — the distraction of scenery, dresses, limelight, artificial birds singing in painted bowers. In Mr. Tree's production of the *Midsummer Night's Dream* an artificial rabbit hops across the stage, and the greatest city in the world is amused. . . .
>
> Art is evocation, not realisation; therefore scenery should be strictly limited, if not abolished altogether; dresses and furniture as much as scenery beset the imagination and prevent the spectator from union with the conception of the poet. But all reformation must proceed gradually. . . . So I have allowed a little inoffensive scenery to encumber the stage during the performance of my play. . . . To hunt four days a week in Leicestershire costs about £1,000 a year, and pheasant-shooting is not less expensive. To give every spring such original plays as the Irish Literary Theatre contemplates giving, and another week in the autumn of great plays by Ibsen, Maeterlinck, and

Tolstoi, would not cost five hundred a year, and might cost nothing, for they might even pay their expenses. And the performance of great dramatic masterpieces of European renown, and plays dealing with our national life, history, and legend, would be, I think, of inestimable advantage. These performances would make Dublin an intellectual centre, which London is not, and would stimulate the national genius as nothing else would — far more, it is my belief, than a university or a picture gallery.

The theatre is the noblest form of art until it becomes a commercial enterprise, then it becomes the ante-room of the supper club, and is perhaps the lowest. There is probably nothing in life so low as a musical comedy, for in the musical comedy the meaning of life is expressed in eating, drinking, betting, and making presents to women; nor does the morality of these pieces gain by the constant use of the word marriage.[5]

Edward Martyn contributed to *Beltaine* an article called 'A Comparison between Irish and English Theatrical Audiences', in which he attacked contemporary English character, English literature and English theatre. It is with the theatre especially, he wrote, that:

. . . decadence irrevocable and complete has set in. It is no use saying that Shakespeare's plays draw because they have been turned into variety shows, where scenery and dresses are in greater prominence than the poetry of Shakespeare. Present him as he should be presented, without all this pantomime, and then see how he would fare with English audiences, whose taste is for nothing but empty parade, where the stage is degraded to a booth for the foolish exhibition of women, or for the enacting of scenes purposely photographing the manners of the society rakes and strumpets of the day. This is the condition to which English literature and English drama have fallen. The situation reminds us of what Rome was at the turning-point of her supremacy and empire. Then her literature and taste began to disappear. The plays of Terence gave place to the brutish decadence of the arena, just as the great drama of England has given place to brutish and imbecile parade. . . .

But turning to Ireland what do we see? Instead of a vast

66

cosmopolitanism and vulgarity, there is an idealism founded upon the ancient genius of the land. There is, in fact, now a great intellectual awakening in Ireland, and, as is the case with all such awakenings, a curiosity and appreciation for the best. This has come about naturally of itself, in spite of the efforts of certain persons and institutions whose aim seems to be to create in Ireland a sort of shabby England. Some have sought to introduce the shoddy literature and drama, others the decadent profligacy of morals so much in vogue in English society. Their labours have borne no fruit. Ireland is virgin soil, yielding endless aspiration to the artist; and her people, uncontaminated by false ideals, are ready to receive the new art.[6]

Alice Milligan contributed a short essay in which she summarized the Dermot and Grania story as background for her own play, *The Last Feast of the Fianna*. She concluded by remarking, 'I understand that Mr. W. B. Yeats has explained my little play as having some spiritual and mystical meaning. . . .' Here, Yeats appended his own footnote:

The emotion which a work of art awakens in an onlooker has commonly little to do with the deliberate purpose of its maker, and must vary with every onlooker. Every artist who has any imagination builds better than he knows. Miss Milligan's little play delighted me because it has made, in a very simple way and through the vehicle of Gaelic persons, that contrast between immortal beauty and the ignominy and mortality of life, which is the central theme of ancient art.[7]

Miss Milligan continued:

. . . but to tell the truth I simply wrote it on thinking out this problem. How did Oisin endure to live in the house with Grania as a stepmother after all that had happened? We know, as a matter of fact, that he was allured away to the Land of Youth by a fairy woman, Niamh of the golden locks. I have set these facts side by side, and evolved from them a dramatic situation.[8]

Finally, Lady Gregory, looking back at the previous year's accomplishments, expressed pride in the success of the Irish Literary Theatre:

It is not for any of us, who have been concerned in the project from its beginning, to speak of the merits of these plays. *The Countess Cathleen*, now in its third edition, has so often been reviewed as a poem that it does not need any new criticism. *The Heather Field* was given, after its success in Dublin, at a matinee at the Strand Theatre in London, by Mr. Thomas Kingston. It has now been translated into German, and is to be produced, with Mr. Martyn's permission, at Berlin, at Vienna, at Breslau, and at Dresden. In America it is to be produced by Mr. Metzler at New York, Boston, Washington and Philadelphia.[9]

*   *   *

Despite Lady Gregory's recitation of successes, the preparations for the second season had not been entirely placid. For Edward Martyn at least, the new season had been a source of considerable anguish.

George Moore claimed he had helped 'dear Edward' in the construction of *The Heather Field*. 'Not a line of the play was actually written by Moore, but he had shown Martyn the way throughout,' writes Moore's biographer.[10] Moore was to have a great deal more to do with his friend's next play, *The Tale of a Town*. Some time in 1899, Martyn had sent Moore the finished script, and this was Moore's reaction:

> The first half-dozen pages pleased me, and then Edward's mind, which can never think clearly, revealed itself in an entanglement; "Which will be easily removed," I said, picking up the second act. But the second act did not please me as much as the first, and I laid it down, saying: "Muddle, muddle, muddle." In the third act Edward seemed to fall into gross farcical situations, and I took up the fourth act sadly. It and the fifth dissipated every hope, and I lay back in my chair in a state of coma, unable to drag myself to the writing table. But getting there at last, I wrote — after complimenting him about a certain improvement in the dialogue — that the play seemed to me very inferior to *The Heather Field* and to *Maeve*.

68

"But plainer speaking is necessary. It may well be inferior to *The Heather Field* and to *Maeve*, and yet be worthy of the Irish Literary Theatre."

So I wrote: "There is not one act in the five you have sent me which, in my opinion, could interest any possible audience — Irish, English, or Esquimaux." [11]

In the summer, Moore and Martyn made an expedition to Bayreuth, but Moore was unable to get his friend to work on the play. In the autumn, Moore was staying with Martyn in Tullyra Castle, and Yeats was at nearby Coole Park with Lady Gregory. Under their joint pressure, Martyn made some revisions in the script, but Yeats's reaction was, 'No, no; it's entirely impossible. We couldn't have such a play performed.' [12] Moore agreed, but phrased it more kindly:

"If there were time, you might alter it yourself. You see, the time is short — only two months"; and I watched Edward. For a long time he said nothing, but sat like a man striving with himself, and I pitied him, knowing how much of his life was in his play.

"I give you the play," he said, starting to his feet. "Do with it as you like; turn it inside out, upside down. I'll make you a present of it!"

"But, Edward, if you don't wish me to alter your play —"

"Ireland has always been divided, and I've preached unity. Now I'm going to practise it. I give you the play."

"But what do you mean by giving us the play?" Yeats said.

"Do with it what you like. I'm not going to break up the Irish Literary Theatre. Do with my play what you like"; and he rushed away. [13]

Moore and Yeats then began to collaborate on the revision. According to Moore, 'The only fault I found with Yeats in this collaboration was the weariness into which he sank suddenly, saying that after a couple of hours he felt a little faint, and would require half an hour's rest.' [14] Apparently most of the revision was done by Moore. As he wrote to his brother:

69

I am afraid Martyn suffered a good deal. He says I spoil[ed] his play but that is an illusion. I recast the play, but not enough. I should have written a new play on the subject. . . . Then Edward said he could not sign it, and he refused to let it be played anonymously so I had to sign it.[15]

*   *   *

In the week of 19 February, the Irish Literary Theatre opened its second season at the Gaiety Theatre, with Edward Martyn's *Maeve,* Alice Milligan's *The Last Feast of the Fianna,* and the Moore-cum-Yeats-after-Martyn *The Bending of the Bough.* The variety of the offerings reflected the emphases of the developing group: two plays based on Irish mythology, both consciously or even self-consciously poetic and mystical; and one play of contemporary social relevance, realistic in manner and subject. All three plays were clearly nationalistic, at least in their implications, and the press and public were almost unanimously enthusiastic in their praise. The Martyn and Milligan plays were performed on Monday night, and *The Freeman's Journal* reported:

> No one who was present last night in the Gaiety Theatre could fail to note the extraordinary contrast between the audience which assembled there to judge the merits of *The Last Feast of the Fianna* and *Maeve* . . . and that which, twelve months ago, attended at the Antient Concert Rooms to witness the presentation of *The Countess Cathleen* and *The Heather Field.* On the former occasion the Irish Literary Theatre stood on its trial, and the verdict was extremely uncertain. To tell the truth, the Dublin public was not prepared for symbolic plays. Even those who believed in the genius of Mr. Yeats and the dramatic instinct of Mr. Martyn, were dubious as to the great and gallant experiment that was being made. The cynics had a good look in, indeed, and during the year they seemed to have quite disposed of the enthusiasts. Yet the enthusiasts, nothing daunted, have turned up again, and stronger than ever. Stronger than ever: that is why we must note the great contrast between the position of the Irish Literary Theatre last year and this year. In 1899 the plays were produced in the Antient Concert Rooms before small

audiences, very largely composed of the men and women who believe in the future of the Irish literary movement; last night *Maeve* and *The Last Feast of the Fianna* were produced before one of the best houses ever seen in the Gaiety Theatre, composed of all classes of the community, from the highest to the lowest. Every portion of the theatre was well filled, from the gods to the pit, and, so far as we could see, there were only two boxes empty. . . .

Certainly, nothing could have been more promising than the way in which the Gaiety audience took the two plays that were presented to them last night. To ordinary theatre-goers, accustomed to witness the obvious dramas of to-day, one would have thought that a picture of the Court of Fionn MacCumhal would have been a very tiresome affair. It must be said, too, that Mr. T. Bryant Edwin quite failed, except in outward appearance, to realise that great Celtic hero. Yet, Miss Milligan's little drama — simply a paraphrase from the old Gaelic story of Diarmuid and Grania — were [sic] followed with breathless interest. . . .

Mr. Martyn's psychological drama *Maeve* followed. Mr. Martyn's *The Heather Field* of last year puzzled the crowd, but Mr. Martyn is incorrigible, and insists on puzzling the crowd still. In making this remark we, of course, only refer to the crowd that flocks to the theatre to see, say, *Charley's Aunt*. . . . We have seen nothing so wonderful in an Irish theatre for many years as the way in which the audience in the Gaiety last night followed the allegory in Mr. Martyn's play.[16]

The Daily Express gave more space in its review to *The Last Feast of the Fianna* than to *Maeve*. Miss Milligan's play, looking back to the Ossian and Patrick dialogues, seemed a more proper way to create a national drama than Martyn's Ibsenism. Of *The Last Feast*, the paper wrote:

. . . it has a charm, particularly for Irish people, which makes up for its deficiencies in dramatic intensity. If it has no other merits, it reproduces, at all events, in a vivid manner the main characteristics of the heroic age of Ireland. It refreshes us with a pleasant breath of poetry, for Miss Milligan's is a poet's

71

touch, and there is sufficient novelty and charm in her work to arrest the attention of her audience. It was curious to see a crowd of spectators, accustomed to the highly-spiced vulgarities of the modern theatre, applauding with genuine relish a poetical thought or a musical passage.[17]

Dorothy Hammond was admired, as was Fanny Morris, but T. Bryant Edwin's Fionn 'scarcely brought out with sufficient impressiveness the nobility of the hero'.

Maeve was thought to need pruning, but, 'It was admirably acted . . . [and] was enthusiastically received. Its symbolic meaning was easily understood by the audience, and perverted by the gallery into a political attack upon England.' Dorothy Hammond was again particularly admired, and the only actor who was criticized was J. Herbert Walter whose Hugh Fitzwalter 'was a little too much of the conventional Englishman'.[18]

The Irish Daily Independent also devoted much more space to *The Last Feast of the Fianna* than to *Maeve*, even though the first play lasted only twenty minutes:

> The scene was beautifully staged, presenting the King and Queen and Court, comprising a fine grouping of cup-bearers and bondswomen, all richly attired in ancient Gaelic costume.[19] The play then proceeds, the dialogue being of a declamatory order, couched in that very descriptive style of prose poetry such as runs through the Ossianic translations or inventions. The text is of an impressive and rhythmical style, but not altogether innocent of crudities. But the whole colouring of the piece is vivid, and is calculated to work upon the imagination of listeners. Some very beautiful music — ancient Irish airs supplied by the Gaelic League and orchestrated by Mrs. C. Milligan-Fox, sister of the authoress of the play — was contributed in the form of a double-string quartet with fine effect. . . .
>
> The piece was received with great enthusiasm. Miss Milligan was called before the curtain, and had to bow her acknowledgement. Next followed Mr. Edward Martyn's two-act drama, *Maeve*. The piece is a psychological drama, which is delightfully fanciful and fairy-like. It is much richer in imaginative lore than *The Heather Field*. . . .[20]

The one dissenting note in this chorus of praise was *The Irish Times*:

The declared object of the Irish Literary Theatre is worthy of the most intense respect and admiration; that the dry-rot which has eaten into the English drama should be ended everybody will agree, but if, in place of vivacity and a relief from care and the seriousness of modern life, we are offered insipidity, dullness, the very condemnation of wit, of vigour, of liveliness — if, in fact, everything that can relieve man from the stress and struggle of this intense workaday world of ours, is banished from the only place where nowadays one can get the slightest reprieve from the commonplace and the oppressive, then give us back, by all means, the musical comedy, the inane farce imported from France, and spoiled in the importation, give us something which means nothing in place of that which is supposed to mean everything, but which requires a bore at your elbow to explain it and its hidden and incomprehensible mysteries. These remarks are entirely intended as a comment upon the impressions produced last night by Mr. Edward Martyn's play, and they are not intended in any unfriendly or unsympathetic sense. Why he should have marred a fine psychological novel — and we don't like the adjective, although we use it — by endeavouring to adapt it to the stage, of which, apparently, the author knows absolutely nothing, is perfectly mysterious. *Maeve*, the play, is absurd and ridiculous, because it is not a play, because it is written in direct contravention of the very essentials of the stage, because it appeals, not as a play should appeal — to the eye, to the ear direct, to the emotions direct — but because it appeals solely to the mind. Fine, logical, consistent argument against human nature it certainly is, but it is not, as a play should be, a reflex of human nature, and therefore Mr. Martyn's impressive work as a play is a complete and unadulterated failure. The man in the stalls it makes yawn. . . . As a play, *Maeve's* best quality is its shortness, and we leave it with this remark, that we hope to read it yet, expanded, developed, as Mr. Martyn can expand and develop it, and without any recollections of the attempt to put it in action on the boards of the theatre. Miss Milligan's one-act piece, *The Last Feast of the Fianna*, really

73

assumed the form of a full-dress recitation of a pleasing and nicely written poem. It has no pretence to be a play, although anyone who has read the story of Grania and of Fionn and the rest of them knows well enough that the cycle in which they move is rich beyond almost any similar period in dramatic materials. Miss Milligan, however, has caught far more intensely the imaginative and poetic features of the subject than its immense human interest, and the result is a series of very pretty animated pictures, which should have for their setting an Arctic winter in place of the warm atmosphere of Ireland. Both Miss Milligan and Mr. Martyn have apparently to learn this — that the mere mention of a few Irish names does not and cannot make an Irish drama, for they failed in precisely the same way to make an interesting stage piece in that both of them are more concerned with the words they make their people speak than the reason why they speak them. Miss Milligan's little effort is interesting in its way, but has no claim for the slightest toleration on the stage. Mr. Martyn's work, on the other hand, defective as it is for the purposes of the theatre, is entitled to the greatest respect on the part of every man who values thought as against mere verbiage. . . . The impersonation of the Fairy Woman in the first piece by Miss Hammond and of Maeve O'Heynes by the same actress in Mr. Martyn's piece should stamp her as a poetic artiste of the very first rank. Never had an actress a more difficult hand of cards to play, and never assuredly did an artiste come more creditably through an ordeal. The only thing that would incline us to alter our idea of the value of the two pieces would be this — that while Miss Hammond was on the stage she held the attention of the audience spell-bound, and gave to two absolutely impossible characters a touch of genuine interest which must have been a complete surprise to the authors themselves. Her speaking of the description of the "Land of the Ever Young", in Miss Milligan's poem, was as beautiful a piece of elocutionary work as anyone could desire, and throughout the second piece she sustained a herculean task with little less than genius. . . . The other artiste who made a fine impression was Miss Agnes B. Cahill, who appeared as Finola O'Heynes, and who demonstrated most conclusively that she has mastered to a very perfect degree the art of

74

byplay which is almost altogether neglected on the English stage at present. . . . The pieces were well staged, and the other roles were sustained as well as they could be sustained by any set of players. The theatre was well filled, and the plays were well received.[21]

On the next evening, 20 February, *The Bending of the Bough* was produced, and, despite, undoubtedly, some misgivings about the author of *Parnell and his Island*, the play was so warmly received that it replaced the other two pieces as the Saturday night production. Its first-night audience was smaller than that on Monday, but its topical satire appealed to the reviewers. As *The Freeman's Journal* wrote:

> The play is, in fact, a powerful, biting, and unsparing political sabre directed against the influences that have destroyed the Irish gentry's sense of patriotism and reduced them to the position of social dependents upon an alien society and country. The veil of imagination is but of the tiniest, and the plot is a history in brief of the Financial Relations agitation in its genteel stage. A critic described it as the "rise, fall and extinction" of Lord Castletown. And though that is too pointed an identification, the dramatist has analysed and laid bare the petty causes and sordid interests that have always lain between the Irish landlord and leadership among his own people.[22]

If the well-disposed *Independent* had been somewhat terse in its approval of *Maeve*, it was able to wax fulsome over *The Bending of the Bough*, 'George Moore's Brilliant Play':

> The Irish Literary Theatre achieved a far-reaching triumph last night when it produced at the Gaiety Geo. Moore's much-anticipated play, *The Bending of the Bough*. The production is beyond doubt the most remarkable drama which has been given to the nation for many years. It satirises in brilliant, biting lashes of irony the relations existing between the Celtic race and its Saxon oppressors, the agitation of the one to shake off the yoke of the other, retarded as victory has been from time to time by the fawning submission of time-serving weak-

lings amidst the class in subjection, to the flattery or bribes of the "predominant partner". The story, which only requires the most superficial reading between the lines to bring out the international allegory which it embodies, seems simple and commonplace enough. . . . The powerful significance of the play in the light of current politics should draw big houses to the succeeding performances. Many of the people in the balcony laughed heartily at the countless epigrammatic sayings in the course of the piece, in blissful ignorance that some of these expressions were keenly satirising their very selves. . . .[23]

The Daily Express gave *The Bending of the Bough* a thoughtfully approving review, although it regretted that 'Contemporary issues are presented under so very thin a disguise, and form . . . the very groundwork of the plot of Mr. Moore's play. These issues become antiquated and pass away, and when they do so what will remain of the interest of *The Bending of the Bough*?' More specifically, the paper remarked:

It will be seen that the play makes two appeals — a broad appeal to the popular feeling on the Financial Relations question, with which Mr. Moore ingeniously associates all the current feelings about the preservation of the Gaelic language, the cultivation of Irish literature, and similar topics, and a more subtle appeal to the sense of tragedy in the frustration of ideal aims and the abandonment of a spiritual mission. The audience, which was not so large as that of Monday night, but which numbered among it nearly every man and woman of intellectual instruction in Dublin, was undoubtedly delighted with the performance and followed the development of the plot with the keenest sympathy. The first scene, showing a meeting of the Corporation, in which Jasper Dean, à la Mark Antony, fires an indifferent and hesitating body with his own passion and conviction by a fine effort of oratory, formed an admirable introduction to the play, and left the audience pleased and expectant. When the humour and satire of the scenes in which the two maiden aunts of Jasper try to dissuade him from courses so shocking to "respectable" people told with excellent effect, and every polished sentence created a ripple of merriment. . . . The least successful scene was undoubtedly that at the close of the play, in which, after the popular tumult following on Jasper's desertion, the dishevelled corporators seek refuge in his house. The language and action of this part of the play are somewhat out of gear with the situation — men with torn garments and bleeding heads do not discuss affairs in their reflective fashion. This, however, is the only episode in which there has been any failure in dramatic realisation. The character of Kirwan, the man who is quietly and steadfastly faithful to his star, though he knows that he can never lead his fellows along the path he has chosen, and sees even those he has inspired fall away from their mission, is very finely conceived and drawn by the author, and was played impassively by Mr. William Devereux, although one felt sometimes a little annoyed by his close resemblance in manner and appearance to Mr. George Alexander. The part of Jasper Dean was taken by Mr. Percy Lyndal, who rendered successfully, though not without a little staginess, the character of a young enthusiast. . . . Valentine Foley, the clever and volatile journalist, who takes the impression of every mind which addresses him sympathetically, was rendered with great success by Mr. Eugene Mayeur, though we do not see why his costume should suggest that of a sportsman so much more than that of an editor. . . . The minor parts were mostly pretty well filled, but the make-up of the Mayor of Northhaven left a great deal to be desired.[24]

Joseph Holloway was less enthusiastic. He recognized *The Bending of the Bough* as a brilliant political satire, but remarked quite accurately that 'as an acting drama I feel sure little more will be heard of it.' Although the actors were from the English professional stage, they seemed in this instance to have adopted an acting style which was later characteristic of the Irish players. Holloway notes: 'The acting was for the most part good, though perhaps too slow, but I noticed one peculiarity — in the chief performers that of gazing vacantly out into the audience and seldom addressing each other; in fact, so strongly marked is this peculiarity indulged in by players . . . that I have christened it the "Irish Literary Theatre stare".'[25] Contemporary stage practice may have condoned an inanimate, dreamlike manner in Maeterlinck and some of Shakespeare, but the practice of facing the audience rather

77

than each other in Moore's realistic play undoubtedly foreshadows the style of acting later identified with the Abbey Theatre. That this style should appear before the Fays took charge of the acting would seem to indicate the importance of Yeats in encouraging such a style. Later in the year, when Mrs. Campbell's company performed Maeterlinck's *Pelléas and Mélisande*, Holloway noted the similarity to Yeats's 'weird, static, mystic suggestiveness'.

The Irish Times was even more distinctly unimpressed:

> A very interesting event took place last night at the Gaiety — namely the production of *The Bending of the Bough*, by Mr. George Moore, under the aegis of the Irish Literary Theatre. There is no one more entitled to respectful consideration than George Moore, but that the author of *Esther Waters* should have signed his name to this production requires some explanation. We who have read his works, and who have acknowledged him one of the greatest English novelists of the generation, placed on our trial as in a sense we are, will say that this is not George Moore's work, and does not represent his art. Having sat for three long weary hours in the Gaiety Theatre, if the writer were asked to tell the story of the play we would be compelled to sit silent. Story none, dialogue dull, action weak—that is the play which an audience was asked to assist in last night. Where does George Moore come in . . . in the wretched attempt to adapt Ibsen's insipid municipal drama, *An Enemy of the People*, to the Dublin stage? George Moore, whose books, however much we may dislike and disagree with them, never had anything to do with the lifeless and contemptible blocks which form the *dramatis personae* of this piece — never had anything to do with the limping plot which in this instance is supposed to constitute an action. Action, plot, dialogue, literature — where can they be found? One might as well ask where George Moore is to be found. Ask anyone who had never before heard of the so-called play, and who was in the theatre last night, to tell the story — story there is none, plot there is none. Of dull, dry, insipid, unnatural, wretchedly commonplace conversation there is an immensity — where is George Moore? The fact is that this *Bending of the Bough*, or whatever else it is called, is not — cannot be — Mr. George Moore's. . . . To approach

the occasion in the language of convention, a fairly well-filled house received the play with a fair degree of favouritism; but so far as the writer is concerned, he cannot give any reason why the piece should be tolerated. . . . How is it that men writing for an Irish audience should think that Ibsen and his methods are the right thing? Against such an idea we most strenuously protest.[26]

Whoever the *Times* reviewer was, he seems certainly to have had more than an inkling that the play was not precisely Moore's.[27]

*   *   *

Despite the persuasive strictures of *The Irish Times*, the more general view of the literary theatre was that expressed in a leading article in *The Irish Daily Independent*:

The measure of a country's greatness is the merit of its art. Now, literature, being the highest form of art, and drama the most exalted form of literature, it follows that no country can be truly great which cannot boast great drama and good literature. . . . And though no Shakespeare has yet arisen to give Ireland drama which takes admiration captive, there is hope that out of the new literary movement there may come dramatic seed which, like the small grain in the parable, shall grow until it spring into the greatest tree in the forest of pure literature. For, in the Ireland of today are many of the circumstances that attended the grand literary revivals of which history tells. Our land had passed, and even now is passing, through a period of unrest. Men's minds are agitated; mighty questions force themselves upon us; and from out of the turmoil and the conflict there come thoughts, and yearnings, and desires, which struggle to take shape in literature, just as the agitation which preceded and closed in the day of Shakespeare bore its fruit in thought which took enduring shape in poetry and prose and drama such as England has not known before or since the vast Elizabethan age.[28]

Despite the rhetorical gush, the statement had considerable truth.

*   *   *

To celebrate the success of the performances, the National Literary Society gave a luncheon on 22 February at the Gresham Hotel for the members of the Irish Literary Theatre. After the luncheon there were, inevitably, speeches:

Dr. Douglas Hyde, in proposing "The Health of the Irish Literary Theatre", said that theatre had now been with them for two years, and if he were to say that it was justified by its works, he should be according it a very small meed of praise: not only had it been justified of its works, but it had been more than justified (hear, hear). It had been at once a performance and a promise; a performance, which he was sure, had come up to their expectations; and a promise that the Irish national genius, working in future upon untrammelled lines, and deliberately trying to cut itself off from English influences, which had for so many years been the bane and ruination of Irish art, would be a credit to the island which gave it birth (applause). The aim and object of the Irish Literary Theatre was to embody and perpetuate Irish feeling, genius, and modes of thought. The Irish Literary Theatre was one, an important one, but still only one of the many agencies which were at this present moment at work in trying to create a new Ireland, proceeding upon national lines. By national, he meant something absolutely uncontentious, non-political, and non-sectarian (hear, hear). The first play they had the pleasure of seeing, *The Last Feast of the Fianna*, (applause), was really only a first representation of the theme at which Irish writers and Gaelic speakers had been working for 1,200 years, and he was convinced that if the play had been played in Irish before an Irish-speaking audience it would come as something perfectly natural to them (applause). Then, again, Mr. Martyn's *Maeve* exemplified another feature of the nationality of which he was speaking. In that play the writer represented the eternal illimitable passion of Irish memory, Irish regret, Irish idealism, struggling with, and vanquishing, the more or less complacent self-satisfaction of English prosperity and Anglo-Saxon smugness (applause). And with what words should he characterise the genius which had passed before their eyes in a couple of brief hours, the very essence of those so heterogeneous discordant elements of Irish life, which so many Irishmen with impotent despair in their hearts had been watching, fuming, and raging round them during the last few years (hear, hear). He believed nobody who entered the theatre and heard that play, and the closing words as the curtain fell, could have left the theatre as he entered it (hear, hear). Amongst the many agencies which were working towards the re-creation of a distinctly national genius, the Gaelic League was not the least (applause). Within the last week or two the managers of 800 schools had petitioned that the children under their charge should be brought up as Irish speakers: and he might mention in connection with that, that the speech delivered last week by the foremost man upon the Board of National Education in Ireland (applause) had been one of the most momentous facts which he could remember in Irish life since he came of age, because it simply meant a reversal of ascendancy move-ment in Ireland (applause).

The toast was drunk with enthusiasm.

Mr. George Moore, who was warmly received, replied: —
I feel that I must apologize for appearing before you with an MS of my speech in my hand. The sight of an MS in the country where oratory flourishes everywhere, in all ranks of society, and in all conditions of intellect, must appear anom-alous and absurd. But I am an exception among my gifted countrymen. I have not inherited any gift of improvisation, and the present is certainly no time for experiment, for, I believe, I have matter of importance to lay before you, and it will be less labour for you to give the extra attention which the condensation of the written phrase demands than to reduce to order the painful jumble of words and ideas, mixed with painful hesitations, which is the public speech of everyone except the born orator. Of the plays which were performed this week I do not intend to speak, and of the plays which the Irish Literary Theatre hopes to produce next year, I only propose to say that a play by Mr. Yeats and myself, entitled *Grania and Dermuid*, [sic] will probably be produced (hear, hear). A more suitable subject than the most popular of our epic stories would hardly be found for a play for the Irish Literary Theatre, and I may say that it would be difficult to name any poet that Ireland has yet produced more truly elected by his individual and racial genius to interpret the old legend,

81

than the distinguished poet whose contemporary and colla-
borateur I have the honour to be (hear, hear). But even if this
play should prove to be that dramatic telling of the great
story which Ireland has been waiting for these many years, it
will not, in my opinion, be the essential point of next year's
festival, for next year we have decided to give a play in our
own language, the language which to our great disgrace we do
not understand (applause). Alas, there will be fewer in the
theatre who will understand the Irish text than a Latin or
Greek one: so the play will be performed for the sake of the
example it will set. The performance of plays in our language
is part and parcel of the idea which led up to the founding of
the Irish Literary Theatre. The Irish Literary Theatre has
been founded to create a new centre for Irish enthusiasm, a
new outlet for the national spirit and energy. This is the first
object of the Irish Literary Theatre (hear, hear). I may say
it is its only object, for if we achieve this we achieve every
object: all other objects are co-relative; for all plays that
represent national spirit and energy are literature, and they are
literature because they perforce put on the stage grief, suffering,
pity and passion, rather than some passing phase of social life
or some external invention which may be used as a pretext for
scenery, dresses, and limelight. And to emphasise this position,
to make it clear to everyone, we are of the opinion that we
should give a play in Irish (hear, hear). I would not be understood to mean that the Irish play to be given next year is to
stand as a mere sign for our project; it will do this, it is true,
but it will do a little more than this — it will serve as a flag to
lead to the restoration of our language as the literary and
political language of this country. But before I speak of the
necessity of the restoration of our language, I will tell you
about the play that we have decided to produce. The play is
not one originally written in the Irish language: it is a translation of a play written in the English language, and for this
choice I am responsible. Lady Gregory, Mr. Martyn, Mr.
Yeats, and myself — here I must break off for a moment to
say that Lady Gregory will be the one amongst us who will be
able to follow the Irish text (applause). Lady Gregory, Mr.
Yeats, and Mr. Martyn were all equally agreed as to the necessity for producing a play in our original language, but I am

responsible for the decision to produce a translation rather than an original play in Irish. In my opinion an original play in Irish would be too hazardous an adventure; the art of writing for the stage is not easily acquired — the number of Irish writers is limited, and to produce a bad play written in Irish would be a misfortune. Moreover, I think our first Irish play has to rest on a solid literary foundation so that it may be possessed of a second life apart from its first life, which is necessarily transitory. I wish to present those who read our language with a piece of solid literature, and for this end my choice fell on a play at once simple and literary — *The Land of Heart's Desire* — by Mr. W. B. Yeats (applause). Mr. Yeats was at first averse to the translation of the play. I never grasped his reasons, but this was perhaps my fault, for I was overborne with the desire to obtain his consent, and he has given his consent. Dr. Douglas Hyde, whose Irish scholarship has passed beyond question, has been pleased to promise to translate the play for us. More on this point I need not say. Mr. Yeats will make what further explanations may be necessary, and I will hasten to the essential subject — the subject on which I have come to speak to you — the necessity of the revival of the language if Ireland is to preserve her individuality among nations. . . .

After speaking long and enthusiastically upon the Irish language, Moore concluded with a point that amused people somewhat at his expense:

Many of us here are too old or have not the leisure to learn a new language. I am amongst these. I am too old, and have not the leisure to learn Irish (laughter and "no, no"). In my youth Irish was still spoken everywhere; but then the gentry took pride in not understanding their own language. It was our misfortune that such false fashion should have prevailed and kept us in ignorance of our language, but it will be our fault if our children do not learn their own language. I have no children, but I shall at once arrange that my brother's children shall learn Irish (laughter). I have written to my sister-in-law telling her that I will undertake this essential part of her children's education. I will arrange that they have a nurse

83

straight from Aran (laughter), for I am convinced that it profits a man nothing if he knows all the languages of the world and knows not his own (applause).

Mr. Martyn also responded, and thanked the company very sincerely for the kind way in which they had always received whatever work he had put before them. This year he was very proud to be associated with Miss Milligan, who had produced a beautiful little work — in fact, of its kind, a perfect work of art (applause).

Mr. W. B. Yeats, in proposing the toast of "The Irish Literary Society", said the vital question of the moment was the Irish language. The whole fate of the language might be this very week hanging in the balance. A new educational system was about to be introduced for Ireland. It might depend upon the action of their representative in Parliament whether that system was one that would preserve the Irish language throughout the country or one that would stifle it. Mr. Starkie's speech was certainly admirable (applause). It was, perhaps, the most sympathetic and intelligent speech which any official had made in Ireland upon any question for many years. But they had seen false dawns and deceptive lights so that no one could be quite sure. He thought that all Irishmen should insist upon their representatives in Parliament opposing any denational-ising system of education; if any such denationalising system was introduced into Parliament they would require their Parliamentary representatives to use obstruction, insult, and every old weapon with which they had met the stranger in the past. And the present was a good moment for meeting the stranger and forcing from him that which they needed (applause). In the National Literary Society people of all politics had met together resolved upon preserving the distinctive soul of this country. It was only their misfortune that the Society had had to work in the English tongue. It was well that every man should know his enemy, and Mr. Moore had helped them in his most powerful play, that whirlwind of passion, *The Bending of the Bough*. The Society was not provincial. Trinity College was provincial (applause). That was why, for all these past years it had produced not one creative mind, it had not produced one man who possessed a really distinguished command of the English language (cries of "Ferguson" and

"Hyde"). He meant in recent years. Without any fear that his prophecy would be proved false he would venture to say that in ten years more of the intellect of this country would be with them, in Trinity College all the ablest of the students would be with them; in ten years those who were now against them would feel the shadows gathering about them (applause).[29]

* * *

Frank and Willie Fay were also busy. They continued actively with the W. G. Fay Comedy Combination, giving many performances from their simple repertoire, plays such as *The Irish Tutor* and *That Rascal Pat*. In 1900, W. G. Fay worked with Maud Gonne's Daughters of Erin, in directing the first public performance of Father Dinneen's play in Irish, *An Tobar Draoidheachta* (*The Magic Well*). Then on 24 and 25 October, the brothers presented *Robert Emmet*, a play by an American writer, Robert Pilgrim. W. G. Fay directed the production and painted the scenery. The cast was made up of the Dramatic Society of St. Theresa's Total Abstinence and Temperance Association, and the performance was given in their hall in Clarendon Street, the same one used two years later by Fay's company for the first performance of Æ's *Deirdre* and Yeats's *Kathleen ni Houlihan*. The single newspaper review, that in *The United Irishman*, praises the company for its industry and verve, but says little about the play itself.[30]

The Daughters of Erin were planning to continue their own experiments in patriotic drama, and on 30 December Maud Gonne wrote to Alice Milligan: 'Before leaving Ireland I write to ask if you will really help the Inghinidhe na hEireann with the Gaelic tableaux we talked of when I and Miss Killeen were in Belfast. Without your help we feel very much afraid of trying them as none of us have had much experience in tableaux.'[31] On the same day, Maud Gonne's chief helper, Máire T. Quinn, wrote Miss Milligan more specifically:

Dear Miss Milligan,
    Miss Gonne has asked me to write you with reference to the Gaelic Tableaux, which we are so anxious to have in Dublin.

85

We were so pleased to hear from Miss Killeen that you were interested in the project and had so kindly promised to give us the benefit of your experience and assistance in carrying them out.

. . . St. Patrick's Day falls on a Sunday and we believe we shall make a pile of money as people have no place to go on such a night, besides the entertainment will be very appropriate as we shall have Gaelic Hymns, sacred songs, with tableaux of St. Patrick and St. Brigid. I give you herewith a rough sketch of what we would like to have, and shall be so grateful if you will kindly give me any hints and suggestions you have as to the best way of grouping, music and songs appropriate etc. . . . This is what we would like — or something similar — make any suggestions that occur to you for which we shall be grateful:

1. St. Brigid.
2. St. Brigid and her maidens.
3. St. Patrick asleep. Shepherd boy.
4. St. Patrick preaching at Tara.
5. The conversion of King Laoghaire's Court.
6. Maev. and her Chariot.
7. Ditto.
8. Children of Lir.
9. Ditto.
10. Ditto.
11. (Suggest one please.)
12. St. Patrick and St. Brigid conversing.[32]

*　　*　　*

The new Irish drama at the end of 1900 was not only bolstered by the support of the nationalist societies and the popular press. Some further support came from an unlikely source when the Roman Catholic Archbishop of Dublin, Dr. Walsh, in a dedication address of a church, referred scathingly to the imported British drama of the commercial stage:

86

Now my reason for speaking here to-day of this necessarily unpleasant and painful subject is that I wish to convey to Mr. Martyn, publicly, and in the presence of so many of the representatives of the Press, what I have long since said to him in conversation, namely, that in my opinion, the only real hope we can have to seeing our city and country rid of that prolific source of corruption that is now freely open in our midst, lies in the success of the movement, in which he is deeply interested, and in which he has from the beginning taken a foremost part. He knows what I refer to. I am firmly convinced that the evil will never be really checked so long as Dublin is left dependent for its theatrical representations, as it now is, upon the weekly visits of roving companies of players, with their imported plays, — plays, the evil suggestiveness of which, I understand, is intensified at times by a variety of devices that would not be tolerated even in London, but are freely indulged in by some of those actors when they are playing in what are known as "the provinces", our city of Dublin being, of course, included in that term. . . . The remedy is to be looked for in the success of the movement, in which Mr. Martyn and others associated with him are engaged, for the establishment of a genuinely Irish National Theatre in Dublin (applause). No other can fulfil the promise of that name, unless it is one no self-respecting Irishman, no self-respecting Irish lady, who goes to the theatre at all, need be ashamed or afraid to go to (applause).[33]

The troubles of 1899 seemed entirely resolved, and for the moment at least the Literary Theatre had the vocal elements of Dublin solidly behind it.

1901

Other than the Irish Literary Theatre's performances at the Gaiety, most of the important dramatic events of 1901 were at the Theatre Royal. A visit, in the week of 11 February, of Henry Irving and Ellen Terry, gave Dubliners a chance to see the more popular Irving showpieces, such as *The Merchant of Venice*, *The Bells*, and *The Lyons Mail*. On 12 June, Madame Réjane played *Sappho* at the Royal, and on other nights Hervieu's *La Course du Flambeau* and Becque's *La Parisienne*. On 4 July, Mrs. Patrick Campbell opened a three-night engagement with Echegaray's *Mariana*. Her company contained Gerald du Maurier and George Arliss. Beerbohm Tree and his company opened on 19 August in *Twelfth Night*, and late in October Forbes Robertson appeared in *Othello* and other plays.

*　　*　　*

Maud Gonne's patriotic woman's organization, Inghinidhe na h-Eireann, or The Daughters of Erin, was quite active during the year, staging both tableaux vivants and plays. In a matinee and two evening performances on 8, 9, and 10 April, they staged at the Antient Concert Rooms three different programmes of tableaux. The tableaux were varied by musical interludes, recitations, character sketches, and an Irish Ceilidh — 'a representation of an Irish country home where all the neighbours gather together in convivial meeting' and which 'affords excellent opportunities for the country folk to display their skill in music, singing and dancing. . . .' The press generally reported that the programmes were received enthusiastically, but one may suspect that some of the enthusiasm was patriotic. A non-Gaelic Leaguer like Holloway took a more sombre view of the proceedings:

> In attending the final performance of the series of Gaelic tableaux vivants organised by the members of the "Daughters of Erin" Society held in the Antient Concert Rooms I had quite a new experience in the entertainment line, and I must say that some take their pleasure very sadly if they *enjoyed* the fare provided by the organisers of this "Irish" night. Is there

not something enlivening in the whole range of Irish song and
story? And if so why not introduce a little of it into the "Irish"
entertainments that are springing up on all sides, and not give
one the impression they are "waking" someone or some thing.
The ill-lighted hall and the melancholy dirge-like airs selected
for interpretation by the chorus during the tableaux were
eminently calculated to put one in the blues after a short time
and the air of ill management, such as unnecessary delays,
excessive and continuous noise behind the curtains, and the
constant coming in and going out of the performers and their
friends into the lobby of the hall between whiles, added to the
discomfort of the ordinary amusement seeker. Were it not for
the real excellence of an occasional solo and the novelty of
the Irish "ceilidh", gloom would have overwhelmed me. . . .
Can't one be cheerful and Irish at the same time?[2]

In the week of 26 August, the Daughters of Erin added the production of plays to their Irish nights, and *The Freeman's Journal*
remarked in its review of the first night's performance:

A truly Irish night's entertainment was inaugurated last
night in the Antient Concert Rooms, amid salvos of "arís",
the full-throated and more resonant Gaelic equivalent of the
encore, when it became necessary to recall an amateur actor,
a singer, or an authoress who essayed the interpretation of one
of her own creations. From the rise of the curtain till its fall,
the dominant idea is clearly, encouragingly Irish, and it is the
old tongue that often responds to the warm breath of Gaelic,
that in moments of acute enjoyment or admiration sweeps
from the audience stagewards. . . . There were songs and dances, tableaux vivants, and a specially written play. . . . Miss
Milligan, whose true insight into the feeling of the moment,
went back to splendid '98, must have been strongly tempted
to betray strict historical perspective to an inclination to introduce Kitchener's last proclamation. If it were not for the fact
that they are hanging rebels for the wearing of the Vierkleur,
the casual critic might be betrayed into the error of speaking
of this workmanlike little play as "of the conventional Irish
drama type". It is true we have heard the whole story before—
the hunted rebel, in whose breast the hot love of country

90

burns, the loving home heart, and the true peasant soul. . . .

The Harp That Once is prettily staged. There is a want of action, it is true, and the scene of the harp air ought to be taken in hand very seriously, but there is no reason why on Wednesday night the full effect should not be given to a very clever bit of stage work from the strictly histrionic standpoint.[3]

What we seem to have here is a gentle review of a conventional play which was rather amateurishly staged. The following evening saw the first production of another Milligan play, *The Deliverance of Red Hugh*, and of P. T. MacGinley's *Eilis agus an Bhean Deirce* (*Eilish and the Beggarwoman*), which was performed in Irish and for the first time in Dublin. The *Independent* reported:

> The admirable entertainment on purely Irish lines which was arranged by the *Inghinidhe na hEireann* was continued last evening in the Antient Concert Rooms. The attendance was far short of what the merits of the performances should have called forth. The programme was of a particularly attractive character, and was strongly calculated to appeal to the national sentiments of the audience. One of the principal features was the production by Mr. W. G. Fay, for the first time on any stage, of a dramatic incident in two scenes by Miss A. L. Milligan, entitled *The Deliverance of Red Hugh*. The piece is strong in dramatic interest. It represents the captivity of Red Hugh and his comrades, the defiance which the young Irish chieftain offers to his jailers, and the ultimate escape of The O'Donnell and the two O'Neills through the friendly offices of one of the guards, who, being Irish on his mother's side, is won over to the cause of the prisoners, and assists them to make their way out of durance. . . . The performance of a one-act play in Irish by P. T. MacGinley, entitled *Eilis agus an Bhean Deirce* was very acceptable. The piece was constructed in clever style, and the parts were effectively filled.[4]

MacGinley's play was a simple one-act comedy, in which a woman is tricked by her son into giving her belongings to a tinker woman. According to the *Freeman*, it 'kept the audience in roars of laughter'.[5]

*   *   *

Again, the theatrical event of the year was the appearance of the Irish Literary Theatre. Edward Martyn, piqued by Yeats's and George Moore's revision of *The Tale of a Town*, had withdrawn his financial support, but the previous ventures had been sufficiently successful to interest the manager of the Gaiety Theatre, and so Yeats and Moore approached the English actor-manager F. R. Benson who had frequently played in Dublin and whose name was a box-office attraction.

Although George Moore was in many ways an excellent replacement for Martyn, his name was to prove something of a drawback. Patriots had not forgotten his early critical volume *Parnell and his Island*, and his reputation for a sort of vague Godlessness and immorality were important factors in the generally critical reception of *Diarmuid and Grania*, the play upon which he collaborated with Yeats and which was the new season's chief attraction.

The story of the Yeats-Moore collaboration on *Diarmuid and Grania* is a famous one, and is most fully discussed in Moore's *Ave*, with what veracity the delighted reader may himself judge. According to Moore, Yeats's idea of play construction was to have their first act horizontal, their second perpendicular, and their third circular — whatever those terms may mean. It was finally decided that Moore would have the last word on construction and that Yeats would have the last word on style. A pure and appropriate style was to be evolved by Moore writing the original draft in French, by Lady Gregory translating that into English, by Tadhg O'Donoghue translating the English into Irish, by Lady Gregory translating the Irish back into English, and by Yeats, after this purifying process, putting 'style upon it'. Moore did actually go to France to begin the writing. 'It is impossible,' he said, 'to write this play in French in Galway. A French atmosphere is necessary. . . .' [6] About four pages of what he managed to write in, as he called it, 'my French of Stratford atte Bowe', he printed in *Ave*.

Both men, of course, were prolific writers and in different ways both were business-like craftsmen. So a play emerged. Nevertheless, they were an ill-matched team, and their next attempt at collaboration was, no doubt fortunately, abortive.

The season's second play was a short piece in Irish by Douglas Hyde, *Casadh an tSugáin* or *The Twisting of the Rope*. This short piece, performed after the long play, was acted by Irish-speaking amateurs; and, even if we discount that enthusiasm generated by patriotism, it seems to have been a most engaging and lively production. Although a chorus of criticism from both patriots and intellectuals greeted *Diarmuid and Grania*, there was nothing but praise for *The Twisting of the Rope*.

Reports of the rehearsals of Hyde's play vary somewhat, but George Moore certainly regarded himself as responsible for its production. He was at this time extremely enthusiastic about promoting the Irish language, and he quotes in *Salve* the following interchange with Yeats:

> "You had better go over to Birmingham and see if you can't get another woman to play the part."
>
> "But our play doesn't matter, Yeats; what matters is *The Twisting of the Rope*. We either want to make Irish the language of Ireland, or we don't; and if we do, nothing else matters. Hyde is excellent in his part, and if I can get the rest straightened out, and if the play be well received, the Irish language will at least have gotten its chance."
>
> Yeats did not take so exaggerated a view of the performance of Hyde's play as I did.[7]

In a letter quoted elsewhere in this chapter, Moore implies his disappointment with the production of *Diarmuid and Grania*, and suggests that this semi-failure was the price that he had to pay for his attention to the Hyde rehearsals.

Also in *Salve*, Moore writes that he desired the Irish actors in Hyde's play to learn their parts during rehearsal. 'And for three weeks I followed the Irish play in a translation made by Hyde himself teaching everyone his or her part, throwing all my energy into the production, giving it as much attention as the most conscientious *régisseur* ever gave to a play at the *Français*.'[8] The following letter of Moore's bears out this claim and indeed suggests that the accounts in *Hail and Farewell* are more trustworthy than has been thought:

> Dear Hyde,
>
> I am sending a proof of the play to Miss O'Kennedy. I have written begging of her not to learn it by heart and I hope you will not learn your part until you have rehearsed the play and know the positions and the business. Much better begin by

93

reading the play and trying to act the positions. In this way the actor instinctively suits his reading to the reading adopted by the actress. In acting we must take into account the limitations of the people we are acting with. There will be plenty of time to rehearse the play but your presence in Dublin will help us. You will be able to help me to keep up the correspondence in the Press. I wish you would send a short letter to the Truly Nationals, better still to *The Irish Times*. Yes, write to *The Times*. I forced that paper to publish an apology; it libelled me, inadvertently, it is true, but I seized on the occasion to demand an apology, and I was very stern for a newspaper is like a dog, no use until it has been thrashed. *The Times* will now publish all we please to send it.

Always yours,
George Moore

Did you see the correspondence about the music for *Diarmuid and Grania*. If not see yesterday's *Freeman* and today's.[9]

The other claimant for the direction of the Hyde play is Willie Fay. It was during the rehearsals of *Diarmuid and Grania* that Moore first met the Fays, but of Willie he only remarked that, 'the enthusiasm which *The Twisting of the Rope* had evoked brought Willie Fay to my house one evening, to ask me if I would use my influence with the Gaelic League to send himself and his brother out, with a little stock company, to play an equal number of plays in English and Irish.' In his own memoirs, W. G. Fay has a different story:

> Mr. Moore had intended to produce this play [*The Twisting of the Rope*] himself, but he found his experience in dealing with professional actors in London of little use in coaching the Gaelic-speaking amateurs supplied by the League. Indeed it was, if anything, a hindrance, and so he finally sent for me to know if I would take over the job, which I was very glad to do. My knowledge of Gaelic was not extensive [in *Salve* Moore quotes Fay as saying that neither he nor his brother had any Gaelic at all], but my experience of producing amateurs was, and, with Dr. Hyde to help me, I knew I could manage. I got all the actors to speak their lines in English first while I gave

the business and the positions. When they had got these right
we turned the play back into Gaelic and in this way put it
together bit by bit. It was all a valuable experience for me because it proved that, given the good-will of the actors, I could
get the same acting value out of the play whether it was spoken
in English or Gaelic.[10]

In a letter written in 1904 to Joseph Holloway, Frank Fay remarked, 'By the way, I don't know whether you know that only
for the brother, *The Twisting of the Rope* could not have been
given. He rehearsed and produced it at the Gaiety.' [11]

In later years particularly, the Fays tended to be understandably
belligerent in claiming credit for their early efforts, but it is probably unfair to deny Moore any significant part in the rehearsal of
the play. At any rate, it is quite impossible at this date to untangle
who did what, and the best that can be said is that the production
of Hyde's play was lively and effective, and enjoyed by all who
saw it.

The rehearsals of *Diarmuid and Grania* did not go too smoothly
either. Moore visited the Bensons in Brighton in August, and it was
apparently with Benson that the much deplored idea of bringing a
sheep onstage originated. As Moore wrote to Yeats:

> He is very much taken with the idea of sheep-shearing. He
> says he will carry in a sheep. [In Act 2 there was a stage
> direction, "Enter Diarmuid and a shepherd carrying fleeces."]
> I told him a sheep is a difficult animal to carry, but he says
> there will be no difficulty for him. The stage will show fleeces
> hung about, there will be branding irons and crooks. . . . I
> cannot tell you how pleased I am; I walk about the streets
> thinking of the fleeces and the sheep." [12]

Later, when the Benson company had come over to Dublin, the
sheep had shrunk to a kid, and Yeats wrote to Lady Gregory:

> Yesterday we were rehearsing at the Gaiety. The kid Benson
> is to carry in his arms was wandering in and out among the
> stage properties. I was saying to myself, "Here we are, a lot
> of intelligent people who might have been doing some sort of
> decent work that leaves the soul free; yet here we are, going

through all sorts of trouble and annoyance for a mob that knows neither literature nor art. I might have been away, away in the country, in Italy perhaps, writing poems for my equals and my betters. The kid is the only sensible creature on the stage. He knows his business and keeps to it." At that very moment one of the actors called out, "Look at the kid, eating the property ivy!" [13]

Nobody was entirely happy with the casting, and the actors, many of whom later became well known, had some difficulty with the pronunciation of the names. As J. C. Trewin sums up various testimonies:

At rehearsal W. G. Fay discovered that they were pronouncing Diarmuid in three or four different ways, and calling Grania Grawniar or Grainyah. Matheson Lang said that, though Yeats was very particular about pronunciation, nobody could manage the name of Caoelte. The company called it "Kaoltay"; Yeats said it ought to be "Wheelsher". That night Harcourt Williams was addressed successively as "Wheelchair", "Cold-tea", and "Quilty", to the horror of patriots. But patriots hated the play.[14]

*   *   *

Shortly before the performances in the Gaiety, the theatre again published its magazine, although the name was changed from *Beltaine*. As Yeats explained, 'I have called this little collection of writings *Samhain*, the old name for the beginning of winter, because our plays this year are in October, and because our Theatre is coming to an end in its present shape.' [15] The issue contained some introductory paragraphs by Yeats, called 'Windlestraws', on a variety of subjects; a short essay by Moore called 'The Irish Literary Theatre'; an even shorter essay by Martyn called 'A Plea for a National Theatre in Ireland'; a retelling of 'The Legend of Diarmuid and Grania' by Lady Gregory and signed with her initials; the text in Irish of Hyde's *Casadh an tSugáin*, and an unsigned translation into English of the play, by Lady Gregory.

Yeats's 'Windlestraws' has been several times reprinted, save for one short paragraph and occasional single sentences, and so we will

96

not reprint it again here. The most important point that he made, however, was that the Irish Literary Theatre in its present form was coming to an end. He also discussed with not complete accuracy several Gaelic plays the writing of which the Literary Theatre inspired, among them were P. T. MacGinley's *Eilis agus an Bhean Deirce*, Father Peter O'Leary's *Tadg Saor*, and Father Dinneen's *Creadeamh agus Gorta*; he gently criticized Miss Lefanu's play for its imitation of old models; he summarized several schemes which had been proposed for the continuation of the theatrical movement; and he briefly referred to the probable criticisms which this year's performance would arouse.

> We do not think there is anything in either play to offend anybody, but we make no promises. We thought our plays inoffensive last year and the year before, but we were accused the one year of sedition, and the other of heresy. We await the next accusation with a cheerful curiosity.[16]

The last sentence he did not include when he republished these remarks.

George Moore's essay was a capsule review of the past two years of the Literary Theatre, and is particularly interesting for his comments upon the faults of previous productions.

> It is now nearly three years since Mr. Yeats and Mr. Martyn explained to me their project of The Irish Literary Theatre. I imagine that they were moved by a disinterested love of Ireland; by a desire to create a sort of rallying point for the many literary enthusiasms and aspirations they saw beginning in Ireland. I was moved to join them because I had come to know the hopelessness of all artistic effort in England. I discovered the English decadence before I discovered my conscience; at that time I merely despaired of any new literary movement ever rising in England. I saw nothing about me but intellectual decay and moral degradation, so I said: "Well, my friends, let us try." I knew Mr. Edward Martyn's play, *The Heather Field*, and his *Maive*, [sic], and I knew Mr. Yeats's *Countess Cathleen*; "these," I said, "will do for a start, but what have we got to follow them?" They answered. "You will write us a play, and somebody else will write after you. One must not look too far ahead."

97

And then began the most disagreeable part of the adventure: excursions to theatrical clubs in the Strand and in the streets leading from the Strand; the long drives to ladies who lived in flats in picturesque neighbourhoods, and arranging for these men and women to come to Dublin. I took upon myself the greater part of these petty annoyances — Mr. Martyn taking upon himself, perhaps, the greatest annoyance, distributing of tickets, and keeping the accounts. I think that this kind of theatrical management must be very like the endeavour of kind-hearted ladies to bring some fifty and odd children into the country for a holiday. In both, there is a great deal of "Has Johnny lost his cap" and "Will Jimmy arrive in time?"

During the rehearsal, I often asked myself why I had consented to waste my time in this fashion; the reason was hidden from me; even now I know, only through faith, that I acted rightly and that if the collecting of the actors and the rehearsals of the plays had proved ten times more troublesome, it would still have been worth the trouble. And this, for some reason that is still hidden from me, and not altogether because *The Heather Field* had been admitted to be the most thoughtful of modern prose plays written in English, the best constructed, the most endurable to a thoughtful audience. It was played in a hall, on a platform amid ludicrous scenery. But, being a prose play, it did not suffer so much from want of space as *The Countess Cathleen*, and it was the better acted play, for it is always easier to find actors who can act plays of modern life than it is to find actors who can speak verse and embody vast sentiments. For the adequate representation of such a play, something like a gulf should separate the actors from the audience, and there should be a large, deep stage full of vague shadows. Green landscapes are not required in Rembrandt's portraits, and I have often wondered why they are used as a background for actors. The more elaborate the scenery, the worse it is for the purpose of the poet and the actor; and new scenery, harsh as a newly-painted signboard, like that amid which *The Countess Cathleen* was played, is the worst scenery of all. *The Countess Cathleen* met with every disadvantage. Here is a list which must not, however, be considered exhaustive: — First, the author's theory that verse should be chanted[17] and not spoken; second, the low platform insufficiently separated from the audience; third, a set of actors and actresses unaccustomed to speak verse; fourth, harsh, ridiculous scenery; fifth, absurd costumes.

The theories of the author regarding the speaking of verse I hold to be mistaken; I do not think they are capable of realization even by trained actors and actresses, but the attempt of our "poor mummers of a timeworn spring", was, indeed, lamentable. Many times I prayed during the last act that the curtain might come down at once. Nevertheless, the performance of *The Countess Cathleen* was not in vain. The beauty of the play was so intense that it was seen through the ridiculous representation as the outline of a Greek statue through the earth it is being dug out of. *The Countess Cathleen* awakened in all who saw it a sense of beauty. I think a sense of beauty once awakened is immortal. I do not think anyone who ponders over a piece of antique sculpture, shall we say a broken bas-relief from Pompeii, ever forgets that keen sense of beauty which arises in his heart, and the imperfect and broken representations of *The Countess Cathleen* awakened in me just such a sense of beauty as I have experienced in dim museums, looking at some worn and broken bas-relief.

The performances of our plays were so successful that the managers of the Gaiety Theatre asked us to produce our next plays in their theatre, and so confident were they of the ultimate success of our enterprise that they offered us their theatre on the same terms they gave to an ordinary troop of mummers. It is more difficult for me to speak of the second performances than of the first, because I undertook to re-write Mr. Martyn's play, *A Tale of a Town*, a play which the Irish Literary Theatre did not think advisable to produce. The public will soon have an opportunity of judging our judgment, for Mr. Martyn has decided to publish the original text of his play. So much of the character of his play was lost in my rewriting that the two plays have very little in common, except the names of the personages and the number of acts. The comedy, entitled, *The Bending of the Bough*, was written in two months, and two months are really not sufficient time to write a five act comedy in; and, at Mr. Martyn's request, my name alone was put on the title page. Mr. Martyn's *Maive* [sic] did not gain by representation, it was inadequately acted, and the idea of the play is clearer in the printed text than it was on the stage. But all who saw the play will remember it; it will flash across their minds, and will become more and more realizable with time.

This year *Diarmuid and Grania* will be given, and though it is longer by two acts than Dr. Hyde's play, it is not so important, for the three act play is written in English, and the one act play is written in Irish. Dr. Hyde's play will be the first Irish play produced in a Dublin theatre: I thought till the other day that it would be the first Irish play produced in Dublin, but now I hear that the organization called *Inghean* [*sic*] *na h-Eireann* has produced at the Antient Concert Rooms (it was in this room that *The Countess Cathleen* and *The Heather Field* were performed), a play in Irish. In a way it would have pleased our vanity to have been the first in Dublin with an Irish play, but this would have been a base vanity, and unworthy of a Gaelic Leaguer. There has been no more disinterested movement than the Gaelic League. It has worked for the sake of the language without hope of reward or praise; and if I were asked why I put my faith in the movement I would answer that to believe that a movement distinguished by so much self sacrifice could fail, would be like believing in the failure of goodness itself.

Since we began our work plays have been written, some in Irish and some in English, and we shall be forgiven if we take a little credit for having helped to awaken intellectual life in Ireland. Many will think I am guilty of exaggeration when I say that The Irish Literary Theatre has done more to awaken intellectual life in Ireland than Trinity College. The Irish Literary Theatre is the centre of a literary movement, and our three years have shown that an endowed theatre may be of more intellectual service to a community than a university or a public library.[13]

In his short article, Edward Martyn noted that, 'There are many movements now for the encouragement of Irish manufacture in all its branches and for preventing the scandalous outpouring of Irish money into the pockets of Englishmen and other foreigners.' After mentioning particularly a scheme for the establishment of a school to teach the making of stained glass, he then argued, 'Is it not time that our dramatic art also should be placed on a national basis?'

Are we so degenerate that we cannot meet this demand also by a supply of national art? The first requisite is to provide a stock company of native artists because the foreign strollers are too wedded to the debased art of England to fall in with the change. This can only be done by instituting a school for the training of actors and actresses, a most important branch of which should be devoted to teaching them to act plays in the Irish language. Now it is quite legal and feasible to obtain a grant from the Department of Technical Instruction for this purpose which is the same in principle as the teaching of stained glass manufacture. It is a home industry in the best sense, and means a vast economic saving to the country, besides being a most refining educational influence. . . .

With a company of artists such as I have described we might put before the people of Ireland native works, also translations of the dramatic masterworks of all lands, for it is only by accustoming a public to the highest art that it can be led to appreciate art, and that dramatists may be inspired to work in the great art tradition.[19]

*   *   *

In the issue of *The All-Ireland Review* which appeared just two days before the performances, Standish O'Grady[20] launched the first attack on *Diarmuid and Grania*.

This story is only one out of thousands of stories about the great, noble, and generous Finn — the greatest, the noblest, and perhaps the most typical Irishman that ever lived — the one story, I say, out of them all in which the fame of the hero and prophet is sullied, and his character aspersed.

And, speaking for myself, I am not one little bit obliged to Mr. Yeats or to Mr. Moore for writing and exhibiting an Irish drama founded upon an utterly untrue chapter of pretended Irish history, written in the decadence of heroic and romantic Irish literature. Needless to say, I shall not go to see their drama.[21]

A rather chilling omen.

*   *   *

The plays were first produced on Monday evening, 21 October 1901, at the Gaiety Theatre, Dublin. They were originally scheduled to play on Monday, Tuesday and Wednesday evenings, and there was also a matinee on Wednesday of *Diarmuid and Grania* alone, since the actors in Hyde's play were unable to arrange to be away from their jobs in the afternoons. Although F. R. Benson later remarked that the Irish plays were not as well attended as the Shakespearian production, *King Lear*, which was to be given by the Benson company on the other days, they were at any rate sufficiently popular for it to be announced later in the week that they would also be performed on Friday evening.

Generally, the response of the audience seems to have been one of enthusiastic good will. There was some boredom with *Diarmuid and Grania*, and the appearance of F. R. Benson with a kid in his arms drew laughter from the galleries. Nevertheless, the intermissions were filled with the singing of patriotic songs, Yeats was greeted with wild applause when he took his curtain call,[22] and he and Maud Gonne were greeted when they left the theatre by fervid patriots who wanted to unhitch the horse from the carriage and pull it themselves through the streets.

*   *   *

On Tuesday, *The Freeman's Journal* gave the productions a two-column review, remarking in part:

> The success of the performance of the Irish Literary Theatre last night at the Gaiety Theatre argues well for the possibility of the institution becoming a permanent one in Dublin. That this success was owing in a great measure to a new departure — the presentation of a play in Irish by Dr. Douglas Hyde — was obvious. Every Gaelic Leaguer, every student of O'Growney, everyone interested in the old tongue who could elbow his way into the theatre was there last night, and the enthusiasm was tremendous. But the fact that the play in English, *Diarmuid and Grania*, was given by a company already well known and popular in Dublin must also have helped not a little to fill the theatre. Of Dr. Douglas Hyde's charming little one-act play, *Casadh an tSugáin, The Twisting of the Rope*, which was presented after *Diarmuid and Grania*, there is

nothing to be said but praise. It is a perfect little genre picture, which, in the completeness of detail and deft precision of light and shade, irresistibly reminds one of an interior painted by one of the masters of the Dutch school. . . .

Of the acting of this little piece, considering the fact that all the parts were filled by amateurs, it is almost impossible to speak too highly. Dr. Douglas Hyde himself, who played Hanrahan, is a born actor. His eloquent tenderness to Una threw into strong relief the fierce savagery and scorching contempt with which he turned on Sheamus and his friends when they attempted to interrupt him, and his soft, weird crooning of his passionate verses was inimitable. . . .

If the Irish play of Dr. Hyde is the most satisfying and successful effort of the Irish Literary Theatre, the play of *Diarmuid and Grania* by Mr. W. B. Yeats and Mr. George Moore is the most ambitious it has done. . . . In the hands of Mr. Yeats and Mr. Moore the story has undergone considerable modification. Many of the minor incidents have been omitted and the strings of the drama have been tightened. The effect of this selection and pruning has been, from the purely dramatic point of view, excellent. It has brought out the essential points of the story, and given it an intensity and a coherence it would otherwise have lacked. But in thus weaving anew the threads of this old tale of love and vengeance the authors have spun from their loom a new fabric. They have twisted the threads into a more intricate pattern; and while the new Diarmuid and Grania are vastly more interesting personages, considered from the point of view of human emotion, than they were in the old tale, they have, perhaps, lost a little of the simplicity, the inevitableness, the elemental character which seems to belong to these figures of a mythical age, and have become characters which it is easy to fancy in modern garments. So far has the process been carried out that Grania recalls recent heroines of the novel and the stage. . . .

Mrs. Benson's Grania was an excellent imitation of the manner of Mrs. Patrick Campbell. Mr. Benson, as Diarmuid, played in the cultivated and intelligent manner which had always characterised his performances. Mr. Frank Rodney was a capable Fionn, and Mr. Alfred Brydon a dignified and effective King Cormac. Miss Lucy Franklein played carefully as Laban, but was hardly weird enough to be convincing. Much praise is due to Mr. Arthur Whitby for his admirable impersonation of Conan the Bald, a character-study which relieved the overwhelming tragedy of the play.[23]

*　　*　　*

The Irish Times gave a generally affirmative review also:

> To Mr. Yeats's poetic inspiration was added Mr. Moore's gift of construction, of welding varied elements into a dramatic whole, so that the play was an admirable example of fine workmanship. . . . Dr. Hyde's play went very brightly. His own acting carried it off with great verve, and it evidently delighted the audience. The costumes were most appropriate, but we have our doubts about the *fichu* being worn in Munster farmhouses a hundred years ago.[24]

The Irish Daily Independent and Nation was kind, but sounds as if it were praising the intention more than the deed:

> In *Diarmuid and Grania* Messrs. Moore and Yeats have produced a piece of considerable power to charm. Its dialogue is of a high order. It is couched in a lofty and cultured key, with many strong poetical passages, and a great deal of matter that will capture the imagination. . . . The play is one that would probably read better than it lends itself to staging. Still it is actable to a greater extent, perhaps, than any other piece hitherto played by the Irish Literary Theatre, excepting *The Bending of the Bough*.
> The staging of the piece is very handsome, the scene on the wooded slopes of Ben Bulben being very picturesque. But the lighting was too aggressive, while in the cottage scene the changes of atmosphere out of doors were rather in the nature of a phenomenon.[25]

The writer who signed himself 'M.A.M.' in *The Evening Herald* found much to criticize, and, as he did not allow himself to fall into hysterical condemnations, he sounded very persuasive:

104

To be perfectly frank, this work of Messrs. Yeats and Moore is a bit of a disappointment. It is very dreary at times, there is a wearisome repetition of sentiment in long dialogues and irritating speeches, and a startling absence of any Celtic atmosphere. Lay the action in Sussex, Wessex, or Kent, call the men Cedric and such names, dress the parts for the period, and who would suggest that there was a trace of the work of Celtic revivalists in the entire three acts? . . . The stage version lands one in a world of metaphysical meanderings, whose Grania argues as if she took out her M.A. degree in Boston, and then Diarmuid replies with rocks of thought as if he were a deep student of Herbert Spencer.

There is too much of Grania in the play. One gets tired of her whims and graces, her whining and monotonous low-toned talks. In the second act one feels it is a great pity she has no children. A cradle in the corner and something in it would occupy her mind, and prevent her falling into dozes before the fire, vainly regretting in a timid, feminine way like a woman whose dressmaker has disappointed her on the night of the ball.

The sentiments, despite the old-time suggestions of fourteenth-century baronial halls, sound very modern. In fact, in Mrs. Benson's hands, Grania is an embryo Mrs. Tanqueray, B.C., and every moment one expects her to confide to the audience some passages in her past that would raise her in the interest of all ladies present to the level of the second Mrs. Tanqueray herself.

One of the most grating drawbacks in this piece is the absence of mobility in the Knights of Tara and all connected with that establishment. One hears nothing but muttered doubts of one another's honour; every man accuses the other of pledge-breaking, drunkenness, lying, or something else. King Cormac himself is a mild precursor of Polonius, who has his eye on every one of them; and the minor knights and others in suits of pre-Christian pyjamas raise titters when they should draw tears. . . .

As to the players, they did all right. As stated, Mrs. Benson plays a long, weary, dreary part, and succeeds in losing the sympathy of the audience. This may not be her fault. Grania is unlovable, uninteresting. In the second act it would be mightily proper if Diarmuid took a rod and beat her. But maybe such methods of restoring reason to wives and others, as the modern bastinado was unknown to the Knights of the Red Branch. It was a serious slip in domestic arrangements to so neglect them. . . The scenery is appropriate, if the first set — a dingy stock scene — be excepted.[26]

*　　*　　*

Frank Fay treated the productions at length in two articles. His general view was one of approval for the plays and of criticism for the acting. Of *Diarmuid and Grania*, he said:

> . . . Mr. Yeats and Mr. Moore have given us a fine play, and, as I venture to think, a beautiful one, though perhaps the characters are not drawn on the heroic scale in which they appear to one's mind's eye.
> Mr. Standish O'Grady, who repudiates the legend as 'an utterly untrue chapter of pretended Irish history, written in the decadence of heroic and romantic Irish literature", will certainly be wise if he abstains, as he said he will, from going to see it. But it is good enough for me, and I venture to think most people will be delighted with it. I cannot say that I am displeased that the authors have humanised the heroic and made Diarmuid a man and Grania a woman of flesh and blood like ourselves; our hearts go out to them more readily than if they were merely beautiful statues. It may be doubtful whether two authors of such opposite literary temperaments as Mr. W. B. Yeats and Mr. George Moore benefit by collaboration, but I do not feel that *Diarmuid and Grania* has suffered thereby.

He also felt that, 'the greatest triumph of the authors lies in their having written in English a play in which English actors are intolerable. . . . Truly *Diarmuid and Grania* must be even a finer play than I think it, to have survived the vulgar acting it received.' [27]

In a later column, Fay elaborated his attack:

> . . . I cannot help thinking that much of the disappointment I have heard expressed about the play is really the result of the execrable — I can use no milder word — acting it received at

the hands of Mr. Benson and his company. . . . I am a great admirer of Mr. Rodney, Mr. Benson's leading man, and to see his superb acting I have long endured Mr. Benson's elaborately bad acting in Shakespeare's and other plays. . . . All the plays produced by the Irish Literary Theatre have called for one quality which, except in Mr. Rodney's case, is not cultivated by the Benson company, I mean beauty of speech. In *Diarmuid and Grania* I am bound to say I did not find Mr. Rodney's delivery beautiful; moreover, he was, like the others, impossible, because he was an Englishman; but he did not, in such acting as he was able to give, reduce *Diarmuid and Grania* to the level of *The Corsican Brothers*, as the others did. That Mr. Benson should bring a lamb or a kid or whatever the animal was, on the stage did not astonish me (nothing that he could do would astonish me), but I think the authors might, at the rehearsals, have insisted on his not doing so. . . . I now see that such acting as *Diarmuid and Grania* received was worse than useless. It was as much as I could do to sit out the acting on the occasion of my second visit, and I only did so in order to once more enjoy *Casadh an t-Sugáin*, which I did, and thoroughly.[28]

Of course, Fay was not an unprejudiced critic. He was campaigning in *The United Irishman* for Yeats and his friends to turn to some group of Irish actors, such as the group led by his brother and himself, to act out the Irish plays. Yet, he was not so uncritical as to allow the Irish-speaking amateurs in Douglas Hyde's play to escape without an admonition:

Dr. Hyde was in great form, and his humour got over the footlights in a wonderful way for a novice; he was irresistible, and the little piece went very well. I say this to encourage all concerned, and I mean it; but I would have them understand that if they want to go on acting plays in Irish, or in English either, they must be prepared to face a lot of hard work, and to remember that an artist is never done learning. And let them take great care to be distinct in their speech; an audience will do a great deal of the acting itself if it only hears the words, and will forgive much to the actors.[29]

The costumes drew some criticism:

> The designing of the costumes for *Diarmuid and Grania*, as
> well as the archaeological researches necessary for the mount-
> ing of the play, was undertaken by Mr. Benson's secretary,
> who went to a good deal of trouble in consulting illuminated
> manuscripts and other sources of information in order to
> ensure the accuracy of the aesthetic details. It may be doubted,
> however, whether the appearance of the warriors in the first
> act is really very reminiscent of Fionn and his Fianna as they
> entered the Banquet Hall at Tara. As usual, the attempt at
> realistic production has not been a success, and Fionn's striped
> trews, the material and colouring of which is so obviously and
> aggressively modern, can hardly be said to be convincing. Had
> a more subdued and suggestive method been employed both
> with regard to costumes and scenery — had a little more been
> left to the imagination of the audience — the effect would
> have been infinitely better.[30]

James H. Cousins wrote the following caustic 'First Night
Impression' of *Diarmuid and Grania*:

> In the first act of *Diarmuid and Grania* the actors fall asleep;
> in the last act the audience do. This is an example of sustained
> sympathetic affection seldom known, and a specimen of that
> 'dramatic unity' for which Pater contended, and which could
> have delighted his heart. So successfully indeed was the atmos-
> phere of the play transferred to the auditorium that many of
> the auditors in their dreams — as they indulged in forty winks
> while waiting for something to happen — confused the burial
> of Diarmuid with that of Moore — Sir John, I mean, for the
> other one is not dead yet, unfortunately, as a dramatist, though
> a rude person might say a nasty thing just here —, and "not a
> drum was heard, not a funeral note," of Dr. Elgar's music.
> My most vivid recollection of the second act is of an aged
> King half blindly groping about a spinning-wheel, and mut-
> tering: "There is no more flax on the distaff." I quite believed
> him; and the authors need not have written a further act to
> prove it.

There was a gentleman in the third act who saw the wind. It was during a dreadful storm in which the lightning flashed like a demented cinematograph, and the thunder was banged out of a drum in such a way as to suggest the "Twelfth" suddenly gone drunk before the right time. Quoth he: "I have never seen such a wind as this before." But he has nothing to do with the case. It is the boar I am thinking of, the mysterious boar which haunted the play. This boar never once showed his unhallowed snout, but his influence was felt right through. There was a hunting of this boar, and the audience were informed in advance what to look for in the way of a denouement. While they were leaning back in their seats waiting for the end to drag itself along, "Ah," said one of the actors, "I see someone coming through the woods. It is Conan the Bald, and they are pushing him along." Then from the pit stalls there came a voice, laden with the perfume of chocolate drops, and it sweetly said, "Please ask them to push the play along also."

Now this Conan the Bald was the "villain" of the piece in a way: its evil genius: its comedy relief: a bare-browed, bare-legged scoundrel who took huge delight in prophesying evil. He was in at the beginning, the middle, and the end: in fact the play was Conan — and bald.

"The fools are laughing at us," said Diarmuid to Grania. It was the truest word he ever spoke.[31]

Years later in his autobiography, Cousins vividly described the excitement of the first night:

   . . . *Diarmuid and Grania* was announced as under the joint authorship of W. B. Yeats and George Moore. The partnership was regarded by certain of Yeats's admirers as a descent into Hades. But some consolation for the degradation of a spiritual poet to the companionship of a literary scavenger, as Moore was then considered, was attempted to be found in the hope that the fall of Yeats might bring about the redemption of Moore. Moments of poetry elicited the whispered exclamation, "Ah! that's Willie." Other phrases were attributed to "dirty George". But it came out, as a disturbing rumour, that the typical poetical Yeatsian patches were by Moore, and the typical Moorish splashes of realism were by Yeats. Be this as it may, some interchange of quality was apparent in the succeeding independent works of the collaborators. . . . The play passed on to an applauded conclusion; but there were stirrings of discontent in the minds of many at the end of the first act. At the end of the second act the discontent was vocal among the auditors. The old bardic tale, with its picturesqueness and chivalry, was evidently undergoing a reversion of the process of bowdlerisation; it was being vulgarised into a mere story of a young man breaking faith with his host and abducting his wife. In addition to this disqualification in the view then prevailing in Ireland, the play disclosed the defects, so contrary to the Irish temperament, of being dull and slow. There were calls for the authors at the final curtain. Yeats, being the less garrulous but more explanatory of the duad when opportunity offered, came before the curtain, and spoke of the efforts of the promoters of the Irish Literary Theatre to break down the "vulgarity" of the English commercial theatre. Some of the audience took this as a subtle joke, and laughed. But Yeats was deadly serious.[32]

Within days considerable opposition arose to *Diarmuid and Grania*, and even the originally sympathetic *Freeman's Journal* joined the attack:

Diarmuid and Grania continues to draw large audiences to the Gaiety Theatre. Gossip has it that the play is not given by Mr. Benson's company in the form in which it left the hands of its authors, and that some passages of doubtful propriety were excluded by the actors. How far this may be true we do not know. If it is true it is credible to Mr. Benson's judgment, and the pity of it is that he did not carry his objections a little further. There is in particular one general proposition concerning women which, however archaic in form, is an unmistakable echo of the Paris boulevards. It comes with a shock on the audience, and is an offence which even the most audacious of latter-day problem playwriters would shrink. It will not bear quotation in a newspaper. It degrades the character of Grania and its disappearance would help the play. Unhappily, however, Grania as presented at the Gaiety is own sister to Evelyn Innes, and the play would have to be written all over again (by someone else) to alter that impression.[33]

Attacked from the right by the popular press, the theatre also came under attack from the left. Standish O'Grady had already before the production expressed his misgivings about dramatizing the legendary stories. In late October, the theatre was attacked by James Joyce. Joyce, then a student at University College, had attended the performances of the Irish Literary Theatre in 1899 and 1900. Well read in continental literature and influenced by Ibsen and Hauptmann, he had begun to write a play which possibly he hoped the Irish Theatre would produce. According to Joyce's biographer, Richard Ellmann, the announcement of the third year's programme seemed to the young Joyce offensively parochial, and so he published a short essay called 'The Day of the Rabblement', in which he wrote:

> The Irish Literary Theatre gave out that it was the champion of progress, and proclaimed war against commercialism and vulgarity. It had partly made good its word and was expelling the old devil, when after the first encounter it surrendered to the popular will. . . . The Irish Literary Theatre must now be considered the property of the rabblement of the most belated race in Europe.[34]

Joyce's remarks on Yeats, Martyn, and Moore were phrased in a tone of brash superciliousness that must have seemed, coming from one of his experience and years, both insolent and absurd. Nevertheless, what he said was not without justice. Although complimenting The Wind Among the Reeds and The Adoration of the Magi highly, he thought it 'unsafe at present to say of Mr. Yeats that he has or has not genius'. He thought that Martyn and Moore were 'not writers of much originality':

> Mr. Martyn, disabled as he is by an incorrigible style, has none of the fierce, hysterical power of Strindberg, whom he suggests at times; and with him one is conscious of a lack of breadth and distinction which outweighs the nobility of certain pas-

111

sages. Mr. Moore, however, has wonderful mimetic ability, and some years ago his books might have entitled him to the place of honour among English novelists. But though *Vain Fortune* (perhaps one should add some of *Esther Waters*) is fine, original work, Mr. Moore is really struggling in the backwash of that tide which has advanced from Flaubert through Jakobsen to D'Annunzio: for two entire eras lie between *Madame Bovary* and *Il Fuoco*. It is plain from *Celibates* and the later novels that Mr. Moore is beginning to draw upon his literary account, and the quest of a new impulse may explain his recent startling conversion. Converts are in the movement now, and Mr. Moore and his island have been fitly admired. But however frankly Mr. Moore may misquote Pater and Turgenieff to defend himself, his new impulse has no kind of relation to the future of art.[35]

In 1901, these judgments sounded harshly intolerant to the point of stupidity; now, despite their ardour they do not seem unsound. He concluded with a familiar Joycean theme:

If an artist courts the favour of the multitude he cannot escape the contagion of its fetishism and deliberate self-deception, and if he joins in a popular movement he does so at his own risk. Therefore, the Irish Literary Theatre by its surrender to the trolls has cut itself adrift from the line of advancement. Until he has freed himself from the mean influences about him — sodden enthusiasm and clever insinuation and every flattering influence of vanity and low ambition — no man is an artist at all.[36]

Frank Fay, feeling that Joyce had made 'some grossly unjust assertions' and had a adopted 'a rather superior attitude', replied:

One would be glad to know in what way the Irish Literary Theatre has pandered to popularity. Is it by producing a play in Irish? I ask this because Mr. Joyce speaks of 'sodden enthusiasm and clever insinuation and every flattering influence of vanity and low ambition". But I have yet to learn that either the Irish Literary Theatre or the Irish Language movement is popular. Surely they both represent the fight of the minority

112

against the "damned compact majority". Mr. Joyce sneers at
Mr. Yeats, Mr. George Moore and Mr. Martyn; but sneering
at these gentlemen has become so common that one wonders
why Mr. Joyce should fall so low. Lastly, Mr. Joyce accuses
the Irish Literary Theatre of not keeping its promise to produce
European masterpieces. If he will read *Samhain* he will see
that the Irish Literary Theatre still hopes to do that. That it
has not done so, is mainly a matter of money. Those who write
and talk so glibly about what the Irish Literary Theatre ought
to do and ought not to do are people who have no idea of the
difficulties such an institution has to contend with.[37]

*　　*　　*

A thoughtful analysis, unbiased by patriotism, of this year's
production was written in *The Fortnightly Review* by the politician
and literary man Stephen Gwynn:

> . . . *Diarmuid and Grania* could not be mounted without a good
> deal of costly stage machinery, so that, taking all in all, Mr.
> Benson took a considerable risk, and conferred a service on
> the people in Ireland who care for literature which one may
> hope will not be forgotten. I do not think *Diarmuid and Grania*
> an admirable production. I do not think it was irreproachably
> acted. But I do think that to have it acted at all promoted that
> keen quickening of intellectual interest which is the soul of
> education. Archbishop Walsh, at all events, speaking for his
> Church, adopted this point of view when he commended the
> work of the Irish Literary Theatre as an attempt to counteract
> the demoralising and vulgarising effect of the theatrical perfor-
> mances which England exports to Dublin.
> The trouble was that when the play came to be produced,
> it did not seem altogether adequate as an antidote. People said,
> and not without reason, that Mr. Moore and Mr. Yeats had
> gone to Irish legend to find in epic tradition the plot of an
> average French novel. . . . All this is not to deny the play is
> well constructed, that it is picturesque, that it has passages of
> great beauty. Mr. Yeats and Mr. Moore have established their
> reputations long ago. But the elements are incongruous, and I
> can conceive of nothing more unfortunate for both men than
> further collaborations of this kind.[38]

113

Gwynn also gave a useful picture of the audience's reaction to Hyde's play:

> How much they understood is a matter of which I have heard divergence of opinion, and some people told me that I did not allow for the cleverness of my countrymen when they were making believe to understand. I can only say that I have seen Japanese plays performed with the perfection of art to an intelligent audience who knew the outline of the story, and the response was very different. I have seen even French plays played by great artists to an ordinary theatre-going public, and the applause was apt to hang fire. Here the words were caught up almost before they were out of the speaker's mouth; and I heard from behind me shouts in Irish of encouragement to the performers in the dance. I never was in an audience so amusing to be among; there was magnetism in the air. In the entractes, a man up in the gallery with a fine voice, sang song after song in Irish, the gallery joining in the chorus, and an attentive house applauding at the end. One began to realise what the Gaelic League was doing — and one felt a good deal out in the cold because one had to rely on the translation.
> However, with the help of that translation — admirably written by Lady Gregory, one of the chiefs of the enterprise — — I made out pretty well; and indeed, one would have been stupid to fail, for Dr. Hyde, though he did not know how to walk the stage, had a command of expression with face and voice that very few actors could rival.[39]

For the play itself, he had high praise:

> . . . it is not a big thing. But it is the real thing. It is Irish, and it is literature. The fun is on the top, and the poetry is on the top; but underneath lies a humour that is not superficial, a pathos that moves us in defiance of reason. . . . If one can be any judge from the sense given in a translation and the ear's perception of the verbal melody, it could stand comparison with a *proverbe* of Musset's or (more appositely) with Théodore de Banville's *Gringoire*. And it will probably be played many times for many years in many parts of Ireland. A national theatre that begins with this has at least something in its repertory.[40]

*   *   *

Diarmuid and Grania was the first of the theatre's plays to use music in any integral fashion. As Percy M. Young wrote in his study of Edward Elgar:

> During the summer [of 1901] George Moore wrote, asking if Elgar would write a horn tune to be played during *Grania and Diarmid* [*sic*], a joint work with W. B. Yeats, which was to be performed under Benson's direction at the Gaiety Theatre in Dublin. Moore, having heard and liked Elgar's music at Leeds, wrote out of the blue. In the end, as the result of a cordial correspondence, Elgar composed not only the requested horn motiv but some incidental music, a song and a Funeral March. When Elgar sought permission from Yeats to publish a song from the play he received this letter — one of Yeats's rare utterances on the subject of music.
>
> Monday, March 23 [1903]
> 18, Woburn Buildings, Euston Road
>
> Dear Sir:
> Yes certainly. With great pleasure. I must give myself the pleasure of letting you [know how] wonderful, in its heroic melancholy, I thought your Grania music. I wish you could set other words of mine and better work than those verses, written in twenty minutes but you are welcome to them.
> Yrs. sincerely,
> W. B. YEATS
>
> Excuse this scrawl I am very busy as I am off to Dublin to look after the rehearsal of a play of mine.[41]

This was Elgar's first music for the stage, and Young goes on to say that

> . . . it won George Moore's high regard. "Elgar," he said, "must have seen the primeval forest as he wrote, and the tribe moving among the falling leaves — oak leaves, hazel leaves, for the world began with oak and hazel." In fact Elgar achieves all this with a juxtaposition of A major and A minor tonality divided among the horns, and with a single phrase delivered by the clarinet. The Funeral March has outlived its first

purpose and is now in the general repertoire of funerary pieces. It is a rich obsequy, fit for the heroic Celtic theme which Yeats and Moore celebrated, and given the proper dignity of antiquity by being cast in a modal atmosphere. The Aeolian mode turns up — as it does sometimes in Mendelssohn — as though it belonged to the age and had not been imported by special licence. There is, too, a magniloquent trio in this march, wherein may be heard the distant tread of the first symphony. Here Elgar shows how two parts may sound like ten. . . . But the gem of the collection is the song "There are seven that pull the thread", in which Elgar unusually refers to the idiom of folk-music. This delicate evocation — with the thread pulled through by violins and violas, and sun-in-water reflected in snatches of clarinet, with a whimsical and recurrent phrase in the upper strings (related to a passage in the second symphony) and an occasional harp chord to give the wash of elusive and Irish clouds — is Elgar's most perfect song. It bears comparison with Schubert.[42]

Of the Funeral March, John F. Porte writes:

The solemn procession has a mixture of wistfulness and melancholy, quite unlike the massiveness, gloom, or frenzy of traditional funeral marches. Elgar has caught a mood of rather touching resignation, not without dignity; this may be an outer indication of his freedom from neurotic tendencies, his spiritual philosophy being unable to regard Death in the light of tragedy or fatalism. It is external writing, however, and therefore has no close relationship with the composer's inner feeling. . . .[43]

And W. H. Reed remarks:

The funeral march is of great beauty and well merits the designation Elgar so frequently used: *Nobilmente*. There is nothing grim or morbid about it and it has a quiet dignity of expression no mere words could possibly utter. Elgar also conjures up a feeling of wistfulness in the listener's mood, much as he does in the flowing theme in the *Introduction and Allegro* for strings or in some of the quieter portions of the symphonies. The theme of the funeral march is simple and rhythmically striking.[44]

*   *   *

116

F. R. Benson writing in 1930 remarked that

> The music was very beautiful, and the play full of poetic thought. I do not quite know to what extent my wife and I were good in the title-rôles, or whether the play was not sufficiently dramatic for the virile Dublin audience; but it failed to attract as much as Shakespeare, though it certainly aroused a great deal of interest, and gave much pleasure to the performers, and the public who witnessed it. I suppose the veracious chronicler will have to write it down as only a qualified success.[45]

Benson also described Yeats's curtain speech.

> The enthusiastic poet, W. B. Yeats, in front of the curtain at the end of the first night's performance, seized the opportunity to indulge in invective against English actors, English companies and all their works. His eloquent periods were abruptly cut short by Mrs. Benson grasping his coat-tails and dragging him back on to the stage. Three-parts Irish herself, she volubly protested that we were an English company, that at his invitation we had crossed the stormy St. George's Channel, and had done our best, according to our capacity, for his play. We could not possibly allow him to step forward on our stage and insult us and our nation. Of course he saw that he had made a mistake, and, like the Irish gentleman he is, reappeared with chastened brow to qualify his remarks and make the *amende honorable*.[46]

*   *   *

Yeats's remarks in *Samhain*, to the effect that the Irish Literary Theatre had now completed its allotted span, evoked considerable speculation about what kind of movement should succeed it. One of the most interesting comments came from Frederick Ryan, writing under the pseudonym of 'Irial', in an article called 'Has the Irish National Theatre Failed?'. Ryan's suggestions were apparently close to what Yeats himself was beginning to think, and they were also prophetic, for the movement which arose out of the Irish Literary Theatre developed closely along these lines. Ryan was to become the first secretary of the Irish National Theatre Society, one of its actors, and the author of *The Laying of the Foundations,* one of its early plays.

117

It is not with any disrespect to the work which has been done by the Irish Literary Theatre that I say it seems like a flash in the pan, a nine-days' wonder, which is praised and abused—especially abused — on all sides, and then forgotten.

The fault seems to me to have been that the whole scheme was far too ambitiously conceived. There is not a public here capable of supporting at such a level such a theatre and on such a scale as the experiments have indicated. . . .

Moreover, beyond possibly supplying models to young writers, the Irish Literary Theatre so far has merely been the vehicle by which literary men of already assured status and who already possessed the ear of the world, were able to have their plays produced which in any case would have secured a reading public owing to their authors' names. . . . In short, the fact remains that beyond, perhaps, *The Last Feast of the Fianna*, the Irish Literary Theatre during its three years has not really brought to the surface any young writer hitherto unknown.

Now it seems to me that with the amount of money which must have been spent on these performances, a permanent institution run on much simpler lines, and going much deeper down, might have been founded. It would easily be possible to purchase or build a small hall or theatre capable of seating five or six hundred persons, neatly, though not lavishly equipped. In this, which should become a popular theatre, there would be an opportunity for producing, on a simple and inexpensive scale, the work of young authors. . . . The National Theatre must be virile with the strength of the life around us. It may now breathe the atmosphere of the demigods, and anon the atmosphere of the cottage and the market-place. If one might venture such a criticism, I would say that the Irish Literary Theatre has shown too strong a partiality for the mystical and the semi-supernatural. That kind of drama has its place, but the National Theatre should be limited by no literary preferences and should let the Irish drama form itself under the influence of natural inclination.[47]

Despite his difficulties with Yeats, George Moore was unwilling to sever his connection with the theatrical movement, and on 13 November *The Freeman's Journal* printed the following interview with him:

118

The future, if any, of the Irish Literary Theatre has been the subject of much speculation, and of varied prophecy. Whether the experiment of three years holds out sufficient hope to warrant an attempt to establish a permanent theatre; what should be the aims of such a theatre; how to establish it, and how to carry it on are questions discussed with interest by many people. No name has been more prominent in the recent history of the Irish Literary Theatre movement than that of Mr. George Moore. The fact that he is something of a storm-centre for criticism lends additional interest to his views. An interview with Mr. Moore could not fail to be entertaining reading, so we have interviewed Mr. Moore. He is no longer a mere visitor to Dublin, occupying a room in a hotel or a "pied-a-terre". He has come over to Ireland for good — for what good time will show us — and is a ratepaying resident with a house in Ely Place. The interview is, as will be seen, somewhat one-sided, the interviewer confining his attention to eliciting Mr. Moore's opinions, and giving them as closely as possible in his own words.

INTERVIEWER In *Samhain* Mr. Yeats said that the Irish Literary Theatre has completed its term of three years. If I remember rightly he says that he may be writing an epitaph. Is that a likely contingency?

MR. MOORE I hope not, for the Irish Literary Theatre is the outward sign of the awakening of intellectual life in Ireland. What Mr. Yeats meant was that the three years during which we undertook to carry on the Theatre whether we succeeded or failed have come to an end. Our success with "Grania" has made the future more safe. We hope to be able to carry on the Theatre. We shall try to carry it on until the nation is ripe for a National Theatre.

INTERVIEWER What are your plans for the immediate future?

MR. MOORE We decided this year to produce a play by Dr. Douglas Hyde, with Hyde in the principal part, and for next year we are trying to get a play by a priest to produce in our next session. I have written to Father O'Leary for leave to produce his play if possible. He has given me leave, but the play is in several scenes, and will have to be reconstructed, I think.

119

INTERVIEWER   Will Father O'Leary alter his play for you?

MR. MOORE   That I cannot say. I shall have to write to him on the subject.

INTERVIEWER   There is Father Dinneen; I hear that he has nearly completed a new play?

MR. MOORE   So I have heard.

INTERVIEWER   And is your mind set upon a play by a priest?

MR. MOORE   If Ireland is to have a National Theatre it must be frequented by all classes — by all who believe in Irish nationality. We want to bring the priests into the Theatre.

INTERVIEWER   But there is a rule forbidding . . .

MR. MOORE   Yes, and that rule I want rescinded. The theatre needs purification. I want to redeem it from the counting houses and the various immorality that the counting-house brings in its train. The Archbishop has spoken against the detestable musical comedies, but his words lose force, for he is speaking from hearsay.

INTERVIEWER   Am I to understand that you are seeking to establish a censorship?

MR. MOORE   Yes; a censorship, and I think I can have no better censor than the Church. I am glad the Irish Literary Theatre has decided to have a play by a priest next year, for I want a censorship. There is no law forbidding a priest to write a play, though he is forbidden to attend the performance of a play.

INTERVIEWER   And the anomaly created by the performance of a priest's play will, you think, result in the rescinding of the established rule?

MR. MOORE   I hope so. And with the rescinding of the rule the censorship will come.

INTERVIEWER   But I should have supposed that a censorship would be resented by you — that you would think it likely to interfere, shall I say, with what you call "the pursuit of art for art's sake".

120

MR. MOORE   I do not contemplate writing anything the Church will condemn. I am sure Mr. Yeats and Mr. Martyn do not. I do not know what the Committee of the Literary Theatre think about it, but I am convinced that a censorship is necessary. The admirable Middle Ages prove that. I am willing, so far as I am concerned, to submit the National Theatre, should it be established, to the censorship of the Church. I plead that in the interests of art the Church may undertake this task. The intelligent censorship of the Church will free the stage from the unintelligent and ignorant censorship of the public, the censorship of those without personal convictions, and of those whose ideas are the conventions and the gossip of the little coterie they frequent. It is from that censorship that I wish to rid the stage, nor is this a new idea of mine. So long as ten years ago I wrote an article defending the London censorship against Mr. Archer, who attacked it. The London censorship is a lay censorship, and a lay censorship is almost futility; but the ecclesiastical censorship would be an ideal state of things. It would confer upon art the limitations which art enjoyed in the Middle Ages. I do not approve of the publication of letters in the papers regarding the morality of the stage. I do not believe in these pretences of opinion, for they are not opinions — they are the prejudices of the moment, the gossip of the neighbours. Not one man in a thousand is capable of forming an independent opinion regarding the morality of a work of art. The ordinary man has no time to think on such subjects, and his spasmodic letter of protest does no good. It only attracts people's attention to the consideration of subjects which it would be much better for them not to consider at all. I have noticed that when these letters appear the writers generally protest against plain speech. So long as the conventions and the gossip of Brixton and Rathmines are respected the stage indulges in the most shockingly degrading spectacles. But the moment the dramatist ventures to break the conventions and to disregard the idiom of respectable circles the morality of the play is called into question. It matters not how noble and how faithful the treatment may be. The dramatic critics are not any better than the public. Do they not all think that Mr. Pinero has been influenced by Ibsen? As well might you talk of the influence that Michelangelo

121

exercises upon the pavement artist. Now, ecclesiastical censorship would redeem us from all this. Ecclesiastical censorship would put limitations upon art, and art has never suffered from limitations. Art suffers from indefinite licence. Above all ecclesiastical censorship would free us from the intolerable censorship of public opinion regarding morals.

INTERVIEWER   You do not apparently anticipate any quarrel between you and the priest about what is right and wrong in art?

MR. MOORE   One quarrels with a fool about art, one never quarrels with an intelligent man about it, whether he is priest or lay man. If any difference of opinion should arise regarding a phrase I should never consider it a hardship to make a sacrifice for someone's convictions. I prefer to make a sacrifice for the sake of someone's convictions than to make a sacrifice for the sake of someone's prejudices or someone's pocket.

INTERVIEWER   Nobody doubts that the cleansing of the stage and the raising of public taste are necessary to the establishment of a National Theatre.

MR. MOORE   Yes; the stage must be redeemed from the counting house. Money is the original vice, and it is the placing of the theatre on what is called a commercial basis that has brought about the licence and the vulgarity of the musical comedy. Every year the theatre makes an appeal to the desire of amusement, every year the theatre is moved further out of ideas and more into scenery and stockings. If Shakespeare is presented, scenery and dresses and songs and dances make atonement for the ideas. Some time ago, I think about a month ago, you published a long letter on the subject of a National Theatre. Your correspondent at first seemed to me better informed than the usual correspondent is, but the value of his letter was discounted by his suggestion that a National Theatre might be run "on commercial lines". He spoke of five thousand pounds subscribed, and instanced a theatre in Berlin, and his letter vexed me much, for it was an example of the almost hopeless obtuseness we have to deal with. If this matter is to be discussed we must begin by agreeing that a National Theatre is quite a different thing from a brewery, and cannot be expected to pay dividends any more than a National Library or a National Gallery, or Trinity College. The moment a theatre is expected to pay dividends there is nothing for the manager to do except to look out for a musical comedy like *The Shop Girl*, or *The Runaway Girl*, or *Kitty Grey*, or for a farcical comedy like *Charley's Aunt* and to run it as long as it will run in town, and to send out companies to gather up all that money that can be gathered in the villages. If the question of the National Theatre is to be discussed, let all those who discuss it be agreed regarding one thing, that a National Theatre gives people an interest in the town in which they live, and that it is an educational and ennobling influence, and far more necessary, more far-reaching in its effects than a picture gallery, or even a library. Although the National Theatre will not pay dividends upon the money subscribed, any more than Shamrock II., a National Theatre would be of enormous pecuniary value to Dublin. Some months ago I raised this question in your columns; I pointed out that we poor Dubliners, overtaxed, exhausted by unjust financial burdens as we are, are not only foolish to buy goods that the foreigners import into this country, but foolish enough to pay, perhaps, £150,000 a year to English companies for our amusements. The National Theatre would be supported by the priests, and would gradually bring about the ruin of these travelling companies who take, at least — think of it — £150,000 a year out of Ireland; and a National Theatre would not only stop this leakage, but it would give employment to a number of young people with talent for acting, for scene-painting, for writing and for music. I have been criticised lately for accepting the most beautiful music from an English musician. I was told I should have paid an Irishman to write the music for me. When Dublin has decided to stop this fearful leak of £150,000 a year, and to amuse itself, instead of importing amusements, it will have the right to tell me that (if I should be with the management of the National Theatre) I must employ more native talent, actors, scene-painters, and musicians. No one will be more willing to comply with this demand than I shall be; no one will recognize its justice more completely. The present moment is opportune for such a Theatre. The National language is being revived. Dr. Hyde's play was an enormous success; it delighted everyone;

123

and, as I am being very much criticised at this moment, I will take this opportunity of saying that I knew how to make sacrifices for the language. I remained in Dublin to rehearse Dr. Hyde's play, instead of going to Birmingham to rehearse Mr. Yeats's and my own. I was determined that at all costs Dr. Hyde's play should be well performed. Everything has to be paid for, and I can say with truth that it was I who paid for the admirable performance of the Irish play. But to return to the matter in hand—the establishment of a National Theatre. The plays performed there would be performed under the direct censorship of the Church. They would consist of selections from the masterpieces of the world, some Russian, some Flemish, some Scandinavian, some French masterpieces, but the central idea of the Theatre would be the restoration of the Irish language. A short Irish play would be given constantly, perhaps every night. I daresay some enthusiasts would wish the whole of the performance to be in Irish, and would denounce the Theatre because it was not. I am afraid these people would cause me many a sigh, and not a little irritation, but these enthusiasts would be useful, and though they sometimes prove a little trying, we would not be without them.

INTERVIEWER Now, Mr. Moore, will you tell me how you propose to get money for this National Theatre?

MR. MOORE It would be an easier thing for me to tell you first about how much it would cost. I think I could manage to do a great deal if the Theatre were given to us rent free, rates, gas, and policing paid for us, and a subscription of a thousand a year. Sir Thomas Lipton spent a quarter of a million of money trying to do something which is already forgotten, building a vessel which no one would live in, a sort of toy boat which is now up for sale. For this sum of money he could have given London an endowed theatre equal to the Comédie Française; for much less he could give Dublin a National Theatre, and a National Theatre would secure to a man much more permanent and more vital immortality than a museum or a picture gallery, or I may say anything else in the world.

INTERVIEWER Then your hope, Mr. Moore, is in the millionaire?

MR. MOORE I cannot say that it is. Money is vice, and he who has got money does not see far; his sight is short. A University would not reach as many as a theatre, whose concern was with ideas, whose ambition was to present life from a high, noble, intellectual point of view. I am afraid it will take some time for the Corporation to see that a theatre of the kind I have indicated would be of great moral, intellectual, and pecuniary benefit to Dublin. But one never knows from what side help may come. I do not think I have got anything more to say on this question.

INTERVIEWER But you have not told me, Mr. Moore, what are your plans for the next performance to be given by the Irish Literary Theatre.

MR. MOORE Mr. Martyn has written a new play, *The Enchanted Sea*, I think that this should be performed. I saw him last night on the subject, and I told him that we were all agreed that this play should be performed. I proposed to him the revival of *The Heather Field*, because this play when originally acted in the Antient Concert Rooms was a very great success. I think the revival of the play would prove more successful. I think every one would like to see it again. I should like to see *Heather Field* performed for three nights and *The Enchanted Sea* for three nights, and I should like to see *The Heather Field* preceded or followed by a play in Irish by Father O'Leary, and I should like to see *The Enchanted Sea* preceded or followed by a play by Father Dinneen. I am now awaiting Mr. Martyn's answer.[48]

On the same day the paper published a leading article which attempted to refute a number of Moore's points. It seemed that no matter what rigorously patriotic or moral stance Moore might adopt, he could never quite hope to quell the suspicions which his previous writings and reputation had aroused in his countrymen. In this instance, the paper remarked, 'Mr. George Moore . . . has been trained in that realistic school that aims professedly at painting life as it is, but concentrates itself only upon one side of life and upon the morbid element even there.' On the next day, *The Freeman's Journal*, for instance, printed an attack on *Diarmuid and Grania* from a priest who had apparently not even seen the production.

125

The Irish Literary Theatre Company, if I may so call it, has been in existence for some years, and has, I understand, produced some good results. But their labours this year do not seem to have in them much of the spirit of reform or of regeneration, judging by the selection of such a sensual and immoral legend as *Diarmuid and Grania* for dramatic representation. . . . If rumour speaks truly, it was just as grossly represented as it dare be.

Now, it occurs to me that if the selection of that legend, and the manner of its dramatic presentation, represents the bent of mind of some of the gentlemen connected with the Irish Literary Theatre, the sooner the healthy-minded amongst them repudiate these gentlemen the better.

The general public can have no confidence in gentlemen capable of such a production as the play *Diarmuid and Grania*. It may be said that they profess themselves willing and anxious to improve. My answer is: Sudden conversions are rare, and certainly some term of probation is necessary before the public can be led to believe that they are safe guides in such matters.

The transition from a foetid atmosphere to the pure ethereal blue of the heavens is not to be made in a week or in a month. The evil odour will cling. . . .[49]

On the same day Moore, still gamely fighting, replied to the previous day's leading article.

Dear Sir — I am sorry you do not agree with me about the necessity for an endowed theatre. Germany and France think that these institutions are necessary in modern conditions, and France and Germany are certainly the highest civilisations in Europe.

In none of the subsidised theatres of France and Germany can such a play as *Sweet Nell of Old Drury* be performed, and I do think, and will always think, that the unintellectual drama is injurious to a nation, that it is, in fact, an immorality.

The Church has always been considered sufficient guide in matters of faith and morals. I am willing to accept the censorship of the Archbishop; I believe that a play passed by him stands in need of no further censorship; and I am sorry that

126

what looks at first sight like an enthusiasm for private judgment
makes you prefer that of the papas and mamas.

Truly yours,
GEORGE MOORE.[50]

On the next day, Yeats disassociated himself from Moore's pro-
posals, and in effect publicly disassociated himself from Moore.

Dear Sir — A phrase in a letter which you publish to-day
makes it desirable that I should define the attitude of the Irish
Literary Theatre and my own attitude towards the proposed
censorship. Mr. Moore makes his proposal on his own author-
ity. The Irish Literary Theatre gives no opinion. When Mr.
Moore told me his plan I said that I had no belief in its
practicability, but would gladly see it discussed. We cannot
have too much discussion about ideas in Ireland. The discussion over the theology of *The Countess Cathleen* and over the
politics of *The Bending of the Bough* and over the morality of
Diarmuid and Grania, set the public mind thinking of matters
it seldom thinks of in Ireland, and I hope the Irish Literary
Theatre will remain a wise disturber of the peace. But if any
literary association I belong to asked for a clerical censorship
I would certainly cease to belong to it. I believe that literature
is the principal voice of the conscience, and that it is its duty
age after age to affirm its morality against the special moral-
ities of clergymen and churches, and of kings and parliaments
and peoples. But I do not expect this opinion to be the opinion
of the majority of any country for generations, and it may
always be the opinion of a very small minority. If Mr. Moore
should establish a national theatre with an ecclesiastic for a
censor, and ask me to join the management I shall refuse, but
I shall watch the adventure with the most friendly eyes. I have
no doubt that a wise ecclesiastic, if his courage equalled his
wisdom, would be a better censor than the mob, but I think
it better to fight the mob alone than to seek for a support one
could only get by what would seem to me a compromise of
principle.

A word now upon another matter. You suggest in your
review of Mr. Martyn's plays that certain changes made by

127

Mr. George Moore in his adaptation of *The Tale of a Town* for the Irish Literary Theatre, were made for political reasons. This is not the case. Every change made was made for literary and dramatic reasons alone.

W. B. YEATS[51]

On the next day, Moore wrote again:

Dear Sir — You misinterpret my ideas, no doubt unconsciously, regarding the proposed change in the censorship of the stage.

If there is to be a National Theatre, I believe a personal censorship is a necessity. I do not believe the ordinary man and woman to be capable of giving a valid opinion regarding the moral worth of a play. The ordinary man and woman are capable of being emotionally moved by a play, and that is enough, but they are not capable of any critical appreciation of the play. The ordinary man and woman are not articulate, and when they strive for utterance they lose themselves in devious nonsense. Nor is it the business of the ordinary man and woman to consider questions that are in the main theological questions, and I do not think that it is desirable, in the interests of morality or of art, that they should allow their minds to dwell upon such matters. It would be better to choose someone to think for them, and the Archbishop, or the priest he might appoint as his reader, would prove a sufficient censorship. I think the morality of plays that have passed this censorship should not be challenged.

In your remarks on the proposed ecclesiastical censorship you have forgotten that the censorship of the stage has been for many years in the hands of the papas and mammas, and you have forgotten that their moral sense has failed to redeem the stage from the musical comedies against which his Grace has so often spoken. Your continued belief in the discrimination of papas and mammas seems a little strange. To be quite candid with you, I do not understand your position, and I should like to know if you are for or against the proposed change in the censorship.

Very truly yours,

GEORGE MOORE.[52]

The newspaper had the last word:

> . . . Mr. Moore and Mr. Yeats wrote for the Irish Literary Theatre, and produced at the Gaiety Theatre a play called *Diarmuid and Grania*. That play shocked and irritated a number of people. Some of them wrote to the papers to express their irritation. The play, apart from all considerations as to the prudence of choosing such a subject, contained certain passages so audacious in the freedom of their speech that they provoked what we believe to be natural and just indignation. . . . If the control of the Irish Literary Theatre remains as at present, we are satisfied that many papas and mammas will not risk going to its performance. An ecclesiastical censorship would re-assure them. But as to the probability of such a censorship we are not sanguine. Mr. Yeats — one of the principal figures of the Literary Theatre — will have nothing to do with it; and we believe the ecclesiastical authorities are no more anxious to revise the plays of Messrs. Moore, Yeats, and colleagues than Mr. Yeats is to see them so revised.[53]

* * *

After the production at the Gaiety, George Moore attempted to interest the Gaelic League in subsidizing provincial tours of the Fays and their company in Gaelic drama. Nothing came of this attempt, and the Fays were soon involved with Yeats. This year, then, marked Moore's last strong connection with the Irish theatre. His own attempts at playwriting, both alone and in collaboration, suggest that the Irish drama lost no master dramatist; and certainly the evidence also suggests that Moore, despite his own confident opinion of his powers, as a director was far from being an incipient Antoine or Stanislavsky.

Although his connection with the Irish drama was, largely at the instigation of Yeats, severed, his services to modern Irish literature were not over. It seems an improbable enthusiasm for him, but we are inclined to credit his statements about the Irish language. He did, after all, go on to write the superb stories in *The Untilled Field* originally as works to be translated into Irish. These stories, together with his novel *The Lake*, may be plausibly taken as the distinguished beginnings of modern Irish prose fiction; and the

129

magnificently witty *Hail and Farewell* was to begin a tradition of highly original memoir-writing which has so far given us some of the most interesting and individual work of W. B. Yeats, Oliver Gogarty, Seán O'Casey, Micheál MacLiammóir, Denis Johnston, Frank O'Connor, Seán O'Faolain, and Austin Clarke.

Max Beerbohm gave a prophetic estimate of Moore when he wrote in 1900:

> It may be that the Irish Literary Theatre marks the beginning of a great dramatic literature in Ireland, and that in England there will be no more great plays. Personally, I have great hopes of the Irish Literary Theatre; but I do not, on the other hand, despair of drama in England. I do not agree with Mr. Moore that Art cannot return to a nation. . . . However, my aim is not to refute Mr. Moore's interesting theories but to assure myself and my readers that Mr. Moore is not lost to us for ever. His, as I have said, is a mind violently exclusive, and present disgust of London is amply explained by the impending production in Dublin. But even if the Keltic Renascence prove to be the most important movement ever made in Art it will not long enchain him. His blazing passions burn themselves out rapidly, and the white-hot core gapes for other fuel. At heart he is a dilettante, though he differs from most of his kind in that his taste is concentrated always on one thing, but nothing can hold him long. That he was born in Ireland does not imply any probability that he will stay there. For the moment, he is fulfilled of patriotism, but only because the kind of Art in which he is immersed happens to have sprung from his native soil. A few weeks hence, if I hear that he has appeared in Edinburgh and declared that to be the only place to live in, I shall not be surprised. And I know that the prodigal will come back, at last, to London, the city which has harboured him through most years of his maturity. I hope I shall go to see his play in Dublin, for I suspect that it will be his only contribution to Irish Art. Already, even in his article, I find signs that his allegiance is straying.[54]

The modern Irish drama would not have been significantly impoverished if George Moore had not come to Dublin, but its first years certainly would have been less gay and less lively.

Appendix I : Anglo Irish Drama, *a checklist to* 1901

This list attempts to give the date of first publication, the date of first production, and the original cast of the significant plays of the Irish Dramatic Revival in its first years. It includes, as will subsequent lists in later volumes, only the most significant plays written in the Irish language, such as those of Douglas Hyde or P. T. MacGinley. It does not include new plays written in the Boucicaultian manner, such as those by J. W. Whitbread, for they owed little or nothing to the new movement in literature. It does not include plays written by Irishmen but basically English in inspiration, such as those by Dr. John Todhunter. It does not, for the most part, include plays which lack any tincture of literary or theatrical or historical merit. It does, however, include a handful of plays written before 1899, which belong to the spirit of the Dramatic Revival.

The plays are listed chronologically by date of first production. When plays were not produced or when the production date remains uncertain, they are listed by the date of their first publication. The cast lists, whenever possible, are based upon the original programmes, rather than upon the sometimes variant cast lists to be found in the books of some published plays. Often, neither programme nor published book was available, and in such cases the cast lists have been formed by a comparison of available newspaper accounts.

Usually, any currently available reprint of a play is also listed.

1894

W. B. YEATS

The Land of Heart's Desire
First produced: 29 March 1894,
at the Avenue Theatre, London.

CAST

Maurteen Bruin	James Welch
Shawn Bruin	A. E. W. Mason
Father Hart	G. R. Foss
Bridget Bruin	Winifred Fraser
A Faery Child	Dorothy Paget

Directed by Florence Farr
First published: London: T. Fisher
Unwin, 1894; Chicago: Stone &
Kimball, 1894; all of Yeats's plays
are reprinted in *The Variorum
Edition of the Plays of W. B.
Yeats*, ed. Russell K. Alspach
(New York: Macmillan, 1966).

Gallo	Mr. McCaul
Firmus	Mr. Magner
St. Patrick	Mr. Canning
Chief Huntsman	Mr. McDermott
Ethan	Miss Diver
Mor	Miss Harkin
Emer	Miss Blake

Soldiers, Huntsmen, Attendants

CAST

of the Scene played in Irish

St. Patrick	Mr. Bonnar
King Laoghaire	Mr. Oram

First published: The scene in Irish
appeared in *The Freeman's Journal*
(19 November 1898), and an
English translation, probably by
Patrick O'Byrne, appeared in *The
Freeman's Journal* (21 November
1898). The entire play has not
been published.

1898

ALICE L. MILLIGAN

The Green upon the Cape,
a Play in One Act.
No record of production.
First published: *The Shan Van
Vocht* (Belfast), (4 April 1898).

ANON.

(Probably Fr. Eugene O'Growney)
The Passing of Conall
First produced: 18 November 1898,
at the Aonach Tirconaill, Letterkenny. Most of the play was
performed in English, but one
scene was played in Irish.

CAST

Conall Gulban	Mr. Craig
St. Caillin	Mr. Oram
Felimidh	Master McKinney
King Dathi	Mr. Larkin
King Laere	Mr. Taylor
Conall Gulban (youth)	Dr. Martin
Eoghan	Mr. B. McFadden
Doghra (Irish Druid)	Mr. McCully
Crudo (British Druid)	Mr. Craig
Ferdach	Mr. O'Callaghan
Malathna	Master Paulson
Duffash	Mr. Mulhern
Britto	Mr. O'Donnell

1899

W. B. YEATS

The Countess Cathleen,
a Tableaux Version
First produced: January 1899, at
the Chief Secretary's Lodge, The
Phoenix Park, Dublin.

CAST

Shemus Rua	Mr. V. Grace
Two Demons	Mr. Coffey
	Mr. Rolleston
Máire	Miss Penn
Teig	Miss Ruth Balfour
Countess Cathleen	
	Countess of Fingall
Oona	Miss Harriet Stokes
Ladies of Cathleen's Court	
	Miss Armstrong
	Miss Porter
Aleel	Mr. Ward Jackson
A Harper	Mr. Dickinson
Steward of the Castle	
	Sir David Harrel
A Peasant Girl	Miss Harrel
Two Angels	Miss Lily Stokes
	Miss Angel Stokes
Cherubs	Miss N. and Miss M.

Balfour, Miss Enid Foster,
and The Hon. Sybil Cadogan
Music Arranged and Conducted
by Dr. Culwick

W. B. YEATS

The Countess Cathleen,
a Miracle Play in Four Acts
First produced: 8 May 1899, by
the Irish Literary Theatre, at the
Antient Concert Rooms, Dublin.

First Demon   Marcus St. John
Second Demon   Trevor Lowe
Shemus Rua, a Peasant
     Valentine Grace
Teig Rua, his Son
     Master Charles Sefton
Maire Rua, his Wife
     Madame San Carolo
Aleel, a Bard   Florence Farr
Oona, Cathleen's Nurse
     Anna Mather
Herdsman   Claude Holmes
Gardener   Jack Wilcox
First Peasant   Franklin Walford
Sheogue   Dorothy Paget
Peasant Woman   M. Kelly
Servant   F. E. Wilkinson
The Countess Cathleen
     May Whitty
Directed by Florence Farr
First published: *The Countess
Kathleen and Various Legends and
Lyrics.* London: T. Fisher Unwin,
1892; Boston: Roberts Bros., 1892;
reprinted in *The Variorum Plays.*

EDWARD MARTYN

The Heather Field,
a Play in Three Acts.
First produced: 9 May 1899, by
the Irish Literary Theatre, at the
Antient Concert Rooms, Dublin.

Barry Ussher, a Landowner,
Student, Philosopher, etc.
     Trevor Lowe
Lord Shrule, a Neighbouring
   Landowner   Marcus St. John
Lady Shrule, Lilian, his Wife
     Anna Mather
Carden Tyrrell   Thomas Kingston
Mrs. Grace Tyrrell, born
Desmond, his Wife   May Whitty
Kit, their Son, Nine Years Old
     Master Charles Sefton
Miles Tyrrell, Scholar of

Trinity College, Dublin, and
Brother of Carden   Jack Wilcox
Doctor Dowling   Claude Holmes
Doctor Roche   F. E. Wilkinson

First published: *The Heather Field
and Maeve,* intro. by George
Moore. London: Duckworth, 1899.
A slightly revised edition of *The
Heather Field* was published se-
parately by Duckworth in 1917.
The current standard edition of the
play was published as Volume I
in the Irish Drama Series of De
Paul University, Chicago, 1966.

1900

EDWARD MARTYN

Maeve, a Psychological Drama
in Two Acts.
First produced: 19 February 1900,
by the Irish Literary Theatre, at
the Gaiety Theatre, Dublin.

The O'Heynes, Colman O'Heynes,
   Prince of Burren   Blake Adams
Maeve O'Heynes (his Daughter)
     Dorothy Hammond
Finola O'Heynes (his Daughter)
     Agnes B. Cahill
Hugh Fitz Walter, a Young
   Englishman J. Herbert Beaumont
Peg Inerney, a Vagrant
     Mona Robin
Music Composed and Conducted
   by Vincent O'Brien
First published: *The Heather Field
and Maeve,* intro. by George
Moore. London: Duckworth, 1899;
reprinted separately by Duckworth
in 1917; re-printed with Alice Mil-
ligan's *The Last Feast of the
Fianna* in Volume II of the Irish
Drama Series of De Paul Univer-
sity, Chicago, 1967.

ALICE L. MILLIGAN

The Last Feast of the Fianna,
a Dramatic Legend in One Act.
First produced: 19 February 1900
by the Irish Literary Theatre, at
the Gaiety Theatre, Dublin.

Fionn Mac Cumhal
        T. Bryant Edwin
Oisin   Franklin Walford
Caoilte Mac Ronan
        John F. Denton
Grania, wife of Fionn
        Fanny Morris
Niamh, a Fairy Princess
      Dorothy Hammond
Special Music by
    Mrs. C. Milligan Fox
First published: In *The Daily Express* (23 September 1899, and 30 September 1899); first separate publication, London: David Nutt, 1900; reprinted with Edward Martyn's *Maeve* in Volume II of the Irish Drama Series of De Paul University, Chicago, 1967.

GEORGE MOORE
(AND EDWARD MARTYN)
The Bending of the Bough, a Comedy in Five Acts.
First produced: 20 February 1900 by the Irish Literary Theatre, at the Gaiety Theatre, Dublin.

CAST
Joseph Trench, the Mayor
        Alex Austin
Aldermen of the Corporation:
Jasper Dean   Percy Lyndal
Daniel Lawrence   W. W. West
Thomas Ferguson
        John F. Denton
Valentine Folay Eugene Mayeur
Ralf Kirwan William Devereaux
James Pollock T. Bryant Edwin
Michael Leech W. F. Rotheram
John Cloran, the Town-Clerk
       J. H. Beaumont
George Hardman, Lord Mayor
  of Southaven   Blake Adams
Miss Millicent Fell, his Niece,
  Engaged to marry Alderman
  Dean   Agnes B. Cahill
Miss Caroline Dean, Maiden
  Aunt of Alderman Dean
        Mona Robin
Miss Arabella Dean, Maiden
  Aunt of Alderman Dean
        Annie Hill

Mrs. Pollock, Wife and First Cousin of Alderman Pollock, Sister of Alderman Pollock, and Cousin of the Deans
        Fanny Morris
Mrs. Leech, Wife and First Cousin of Alderman Leech, Sister of Alderman Pollock, and Cousin of the Deans
      Dorothy Hammond
Macnee, Caretaker of the
  Town Hall   Franklin Walford
A Waiter at the Hotel
       William P. Kelly
Directed by George Moore
First published: London: T. Fisher Unwin, 1900; a slightly different version was also published in the same year, Chicago: Herbert S. Stone, 1900; the two versions are collated in the edition edited by William J. Feeney, and published as Volume III of the Irish Drama Series of De Paul University, Chicago, 1969.

ALICE L. MILLIGAN
Oisin in Tir-Nan-Oig, a Legendary Play in Verse in One Act, Part Two of a Trilogy of which *The Last Feast of the Fianna* is Part One.
No record of production.
First published: In *The Daily Express* (7 October 1899, and 14 October 1899); reprinted in *Sinn Féin* (23 January 1909).

ALICE L. MILLIGAN
Oisin and Padraic, a Legendary Play in Verse in One Act, Part Three of the above-mentioned Trilogy.
No record of production.
First published: In *The Daily Express* (4 November 1899, and 11 November 1899); reprinted in *Sinn Féin* (20 February 1909).

1901

P. T. MAC FHIONNLAOICH (P. T. MacGINLEY)

Eilis agus an Bhean Déirce, a Comedy in Irish in One Act. The date of first production is uncertain. The first production in Dublin, and probably the second production of the play, was on 27 August 1901, by the Daughters of Erin at the Antient Concert Rooms.

CAST

(Of the revival on 31 October 1901. Probably the same as the original cast.)

Eilis   Máire T. Ní Cuinn (Máire T. Quinn)
Concubar, a mac
    Proinsias Mac Siubhlaig (Frank Walker)
Meadba, bean déirce
    Máire Ní Perols
Directed by W. G. and F. J. Fay
First published: In *Miondrámanna*. Baile Atha Cliath: Connradh na Gaedhilge, 1902; a translation by Mrs. Sheila O'Rourke and Father Patrick Corkell appears in *Lost Plays of the Irish Renaissance*, eds. Robert Hogan and James Kilroy (Dixon, California: Proscenium Press, 1970), pp. 17-21.

ALICE L. MILLIGAN

The Harp That Once, a Play in Two Acts. First produced: 26 August 1901, for the Daughters of Erin, by the Ormonde Dramatic Society, at the Antient Concert Rooms, Dublin.

CAST

Denis Lynch, a Fugitive Patriot
    J. Dudley Digges
Captain Coverdale, Hussar, in Command of a Company
    E. O'Higgins
Lieutenant Farmer, Officer of Hussars   Brian Callender
Nancy Kelly, Lady O'Brien's Housekeeper   Alice L. Milligan

Polly   Miss J. Meagher
Lady Selina O'Brien   Sara Allgood
Mabel, her Stepdaughter
    Máire T. Quinn
Directed by W. G. and F. J. Fay
No record of publication.

ALICE L. MILLIGAN

The Deliverance of Red Hugh a Dramatic Incident in Two Scenes. First produced: 27 August 1901, for the Daughters of Erin, by the Ormonde Dramatic Society, at the Antient Concert Rooms, Dublin.

CAST

Red Hugh O'Donnell
    J. Dudley Digges
Art O'Neill   Patrick Bradley
Henry O'Neill   Michael J. Quinn
The Governor of Dublin Castle
    Peter White
An Officer   P. J. Kelly
Pierce   Thomas S. Cuffe
Martin   F. J. Fay
Directed by W. G. Fay
First published: In 'St. Patrick's Day Double Number' of *The Weekly Freeman* (13 March 1902), both in English and in Irish.

JOSEPH P. COLLUMB (PADRAIC COLUM)

The Children of Lir, a Poetic Tragedy in One Act. No record of production. First published: In *Irish Weekly Independent and Nation* (14 September 1901), reprinted in *The Journal of Irish Literature*, Vol. II, No. 1, (January 1973).

GEORGE MOORE AND W. B. YEATS

Diarmuid and Grania a Play in Three Acts. First produced: 21 October 1901, by F. R. Benson's Company, for the Irish Literary Theatre, at the Gaiety Theatre, Dublin.

135

King Cormac   Alfred Brydone
Finn MacCoole   Frank Rodney
Diarmuid   F. R. Benson
His Chief Men:
  Goll   Charles Bibby
  Usheen   Henry Ainley
  Caoilte   E. Harcourt Williams
Spearmen:
  Fergus   G. Wallace Johnstone
  Fathna   Walter Hampden
  Griffan   Stuart Edgar
Niall, a Head Servant
                     Matheson Lang
Conan the Bald, One of the
  Fianna   Arthur Whitby
An Old Man   H. O. Nicholson
A Shepherd   Mr. Owen
A Boy   Ella Tarrant
A Young Man   Jean Mackinlay
Grania, the King's Daughter
                   Mrs. F. R. Benson
Laban, an Old Druidess
                    Lucy Franklein
Directed by F. R. Benson
Special Music Written by
    Dr. Edward Elgar
First published: In *The Dublin
Magazine* (April-June 1951); re-
printed in *The Variorum Plays*.

DOUGLAS HYDE

(from a Scenario by Lady Gregory)
Casadh an tSugáin, a Comedy in
One Act, translated by Lady Gre-
gory as *The Twisting of the Rope*.
First produced: 21 October 1901,
by the Keating Branch of the
Gaelic League, for the Irish Liter-
ary Theatre, at the Gaiety Theatre,
Dublin.

CAST

Hanrahan, a Wandering Poet
                     Douglas Hyde
Sheamus O'Heran, Engaged to
  Oona   Tadhg O'Donoghue
Maurya, the Woman of the
  House   Eibhlin O'Donovan
Sheela, a Neighbour
                   Frances Sullivan
Oona, Maurya's Daughter
                   Miss O'Kennedy
Neighbours and a Piper

(In the 31 October 1904 revival,
Eamonn Ceannt played the Piper.)

Directed by George Moore
    with W. G. Fay

First published: In *Samhain*
(October 1901); first book publi-
cation, in English, in *Poets and
Dreamers: Studies and Transla-
tions from the Irish* by Lady Gre-
gory (Dublin: Hodges, Figgis &
Co. Ltd., and London: John Mur-
ray, 1903); first separate publica-
tion, in Irish and English (Baile
Atha Cliath; An Cló-Cumann,
1905); and there have been two
recent reprints of *Poets and
Dreamers* — one by the Kennikat
Press (Port Washington, New
York, 1967), and one in the Coole
Edition of Lady Gregory's Works
(Gerrards Cross: Colin Smythe
Ltd., 1971).

Appendix II

In *The Freeman's Journal* for 20 November 1898, was printed the following scene which had been played at the Aonach Tir Conaill in Letterkenny, and which was apparently the first dramatic representation in the Irish language.

CONALL GULBAN
Roibh-Rádh

Tógamuid teampall mar is cóir dúinn é
In onóir Adhamhnáin, patrún Dún na nGall;
Ardóchamaoid a n-diú, le congnamh Dé
Sean-chlú, Tír-Chonaill — is dílis dúmu gach ball,
Gach cnoc, gach crois, gach cailseán as gach coill
'O Aileach árd na Rígh go gleann dubh Coluimchill'
Is iomdha ollamh, oide, laoch 'gus naomh
For beó i gcuimhne linn i mbaile 'gus i dtír,
Acht cia d'fhág ainm in a dhiaigh ariamh
Ar stair na h-Eireann chomh pésdomeamhail a's fíor
Le Conall Gulban, sinnsear saor ár gclann,
Thug cliú d'ár dtír 'gus do gach duine ann?
Is fada Conall ins an gcill 'na luidhe
Faoi 'n gcréafóig throim 'sta athrughadh mor
Ar fhear 's ar nós 'gus ar gach uile ní
O mhair a riaghail san tír, acht fós tá glór
'Gus blas na Gaeilge in gach béal go binn
Mar chluinfidh sibh anois ag éisteacht linn,
Ar sun na míle bliadhain agus níos mó
Tiocfaidh Conall Gulban rómhaibh anocht,
I gculaidh 'gus i mbéas na n-aois fadó
'Gus guidhim-se bhur gcarthannacht d'ár n-imirt bhoicht!

AMHARC VI — TEAMHAIR

Tigeann Pádraic isteach le fear iomchaire na croise.

PÁDRAIC   Beannacht Dé air a bhfuil annso! Dhuit-se, a Rígh,
                 Agus d'Eirinn uile faoi do riaghail,
                 Bheirim beannacht agus teachtaireacht mhór
                 O'm Mhaighistir mhaith, mo Thirgeanna agus mo Rígh.

LAOGHAIRE   Is teachdaire 'gus ní sagart thú, mar sin.
                 Cia h-é do Rígh; cad í an teachdaireacht
                 Bheireann tú chugainn?

CRÚDO   Labhrann sé i gcosamhlachdaibh.
          Is sé a Rígh an Dia adhrann sé.

PÁDRAIC   Tá sóisgéal liom a líonas suas gach aoin
          Le síothcháin agus sólas thig ó neamh amháin.
          Is sé mo Rígh mo Dhia, árd-Rígh na bhflaitheas;
          Is sé Rígh na Rightheadh, agus Flaith na bhfláith.
          Ní coimh thigheach an guth so daoibh go léir;
          Acht ina seachránacht do chaill na Gaedhil
          A n-eólas air; acht tá a ghuth ós árd
          Ag mothughadh maithe in bhúr measg go fóill.
          O'n aimsir úd do labhair mo Dhia libh
          Tré béalaibh móráin fáidh, 'gus chuir sé síos
          A mhac ó neamh — sin é an t-Iosa Chríost
          Fá-n mian liom cáint a dhéanamh libh anocht —
          An Críosd a chomhnuigh linn; an Críosd a d'éag
          Ionnus go mbéidheadh sinn béo; a's tr' éis a bháis
          Go sdiúirfeadh Seisean slán go flaitheas Dé
          Na daoine lean a theagasg 'gus a riaghail.
          Sin é an fáth a dtáinic mé anocht
          Le cúireadh dhílis daoibh, a chlann na nGaedheal,
          A theacht air ais faoi dhlighthibh fíora Dé.

LAOGHAIRE   An bhfaca tú na fáidhe móra so?
          An bhfaca tú an Críost-se ar do chan tú?
          Nó bhfuil aon chinnteacht agat ar a gcúmhacht?

PÁDRAIC   An bhfaca tú, a Rígh Cormac maith MacAirt,
          A riaghlaigh seal i dTeamhair móir na Midhe?
          Ar aithin tú Mac Neasa mhair 'na Rígh
          I gCúige Uladh céadta bliadhain ó shoin?
          An bhfaca tusa Ailp na mullach mbán
          A Chonnaire bás Rígh Dhathí chrodha chaoin?

LAOGHAIRE   Ní fhacamar na righte so ariamh,
          Nó Ailp an tsneachda, acht bheir fiadhnaisídhe
          'Gus sgríbhinnidhe ró-fhior a gcunntais dúinn
          Gur mhair a leitheid ann.

PÁDRAIC   Eist liom, a Rígh,
          Tá'n sneachda bán ar mhullach mhaol na h-Ailp
          Ag féachaint síos ar thalaimh ghlais Iodáilte
          'Nna susdheann cathair chlúdhamhail na Róimh!
          Fá'n am 'n ar chómhnuigh Conchobar caomh Mac Nessa
          'Na rígh le neart in Uladh dubh na mbeann,
          Do tháinic iomad fiadhnaise go dtí 'n Róimh
          A chómhnuigh seal le Críost 'gus chonnairc siad
          A chúmhacht 'gus a bhás, a árdughadh suas ar Neamh;
          'Gus chonghaigh siad go cúramach 'na gceann

An stair a bhaineas leis an am fadó —
Is focla fiadhnais' as gach sgríbhinn díobh
Tá againne a ndiú; is dearbhadh iad
Ar rúnaibh Dé innseochaidh mé anois
Do Dhraoithibh Eireann tá annso i láthair
Má's mian leó fios an fhirinn fhághail.

CRÚDO   Ní'l sé in do chumas, a ghear aindia
Na neithe uile so do dhearbhadh dhúinn.
Chuirfeá ar gcúl go deó an t-adhradh mór
A bhéirimuid do ghealach, gréin, a's réalt.
'Smar mhalairt, mhúinfeá dhúinn do chreideamh úr.
Seadh, sheas mé 'stigh i gcroidhe na Róimhe féin
'Gus chualidhe mé ó sheanmóntaidhe do Chríost
Go bhfuil aon Dia agaibh, agus triúr in aon —
Ní féidir do na neithibh sin a bheith.

PÁDRAIC   Tá 'n chrian, an ghealach a's gach réalt 'san spéir
A lasadh suas an t-slíghe go flaitheas árd;
Is sian an coiscéim buin ná staidhridh óir
A ritheas suas go cathaoir Ríoghda Dé;
Mar theachdaire lionnireach insan spéir atáid
A labhras linn an soisgéal go ó'n Rígh.
Ma thigeann, a Mhaolaithne eachlach ríoghamhail
Go geataidh móra Theamhrach, a' bhfaghann sé
An t-urraim 'gus an t-onóir gheabhas Rígh?

MAOLAITHNE Ní gheibheann sé acht onóir teach daire —
[B'eas oaóis an Tach rígh píos mó thabhairt dó.

PÁDRAIC   Is é as ondhi do Rígh na bhflaitheas]*
Urraim Dé a thabhairt do lonnradh neimhe;
Oir ní'l 'san ghréin 'sna réaltaibh nó 'san rae
Acht néithe beaga bheireann cunntas dúinn
Ar chúmhacht agus ghlóir móir an Té
A riaghlaigheas iad-san in a slíghe gach lá.
Tráchtann an Draoi fá rúnaibh chreidimh Chríosd,
Acht tabhradh seisean míniughadh dúinn ar dtús
Ar thairngearachd no nDraoitheadh dúbhairt go mbéidheadh
Lámh bhuaidheach ag an Ghaedheal 'san am the la teacht
I dtírchibh bhfad i gcéin. Cá bhfuil no buadha so?
Cia h-iad na Draoithe? Cá h-as a dtáinic siad?
Ní'l freagra agaibh-se, acht éistidh liom:
Ní'l leis an gclaidheamh nó 'n lann nó tréanas lámh
A bhainfeas clann na h-Eireann cúmhacht mhór
Acht geóbhaidh siad a réim faoi bhrat na croise,
'Gá iomchar leó ó thráighibh loma?
Go sléibhtibh Appinin, le congnadh Dé —
Le congnadh Dé i n-aon, 'gus aon i dtrí.

*Two illegible lines. The material within brackets is a guess.

CRÚDO Aon Dia fíor, acht triúr Dé in aon! —
Cé'n inntinn fir a thuigeas cáint mar shin?
Ní féidir leis a leithid so a beith.

PÁDRAIC An measann tú gur thuig aon fhear ariamh
Mar déanann Nádúir mhór a h-obair féin?
Acht fós tá 'n obair déanta léi gach lá.
Fosglann sí gach dhuille 'gus gach bláth,
Cad mar is féidir leis an phóirín bheag
Bhrígh freimhe, croinne, craoibhe bheith 'na lár?
Féach an tseamróg so do fhásas faoi do chois
Tá réidh le freagra ar do cheist anois.
Ní'l ar an tseamróig sin acht duille amháin
Acht ins an duille sin tá triúr go beacht.
'Gus ní'l aon áit 'san dtír nach bhfásann sí.
Mar sin béidh creideamh fíor na Trionóide.
Ar bun gan mhoill ar fud na h-Inse Fáil
'Gus béarfaidh class na h-Eireann onóir mhór
Do'n t-seomróig ghil, óir sé an glas a bhéadheas
'Na dhath ar bhrat a gcineadh sin go bráth,
Is cuma c'áit 'san domhan a gcasfar iad.
A phrionnsaidh 'sa a mhná uaisle tá annso,
Ma's mian libh fírinne an chreidimh fhághail
A thug mé in bhur measg, tar liom go léir,
Oir ar an léana mín úd thios anois
Tá 'n pobal mór a fanacht ar an sgéal
A líonfas a n-anámaibh le grása Dé.

EITHNE A Phádraic, rachfamaoid le h-éisteacht leat.

DUBTHACH Leanfamaoid;

EOGAN Eisteochamaoid.

MOR Creid-fimid.

CRÚDO A rígh, a rígh! seachain an sagart-se,
'S ná leig tú féin go síorruidhe in a chómhair!

(*Exeunt omnes acht na Draoithe agus Laoghaire.*)

IAR-RADH

CONALL An aisling a bhí orm nó 'n bhfaca mé
An t-am 'na raibh mé óg a'r lásoin luath?
Dar liom go raibh me 'rís i seilg fiadh,

140

'S ar siubhal le Dathí thar an t-sáile mór?
Gur sheas mé rís i dTeamhair lá's Pádraic ann
Ag faghail an bhaisdidh naomhtha ó n-a láimh
Ag Eas Aoidh Ruaidh. An aisling a bhí ann,
Ta sgaptha 'nois mar chéo?

CAILLÍN   Má b'aisling í
Níor imthigh sí gan sólas. Nach cuimhneach
Leat geall Phádraic?

CONALL   Is sé an geall so
Bheir sólas do mo chroidhe. Tá mo mhuintir
'Gus mo cháirde lá fada ins an uaigh
Acht tá a gclass-san beó n'ar measg go fóill
I ngleanntaigh dubha doracha Tír Chonaill
Shíos ar mhaighibh míne Loch Súlidhe,
Air fud na Rosann 'gus i sean-Ghaoth Dóbhair.
Mar bheidheadh in aisling chím an t-am a' teacht,
Na m-béidh an chrois go h-árd ar iomad cill
O mhullach Eargail go spincthibh Sléibhe Liag,
Is iomdha naomh ar laoch de chineál Chonaill
A dhíonfas ballaidh beannuighthe Dhúin na nGall.
'San am le theacht; fad, fada romhainn
Chidhim teampoil ghlórmhar ag á thógbhail suas
I Leitir Cheannainn a' cur i n-úmhail do'n t-saoghal
Go bhfuil clann cródha Chonaill cuimhneach ar a nDia.
Slán leis an am tá thart, slán libh, mo ghaol,
Tá 'g éirigh suas arís ós cómhair mo shúil!
Tá mise réidh anois le dul o'n t-saoghal,
Tá 'n ola déighionnach 'gus an uaigh ag fuireacht.
Tá Dia cúmachtach agus Pádraic mór
Le cloinn Thír-Chonaill 'lig a coimhéad mar is cóir.

Críoch.

Under the title of 'The Tara Scene in English', the following partial
translation appeared in *The Freeman's Journal* of 21 November:

*(A solemn chant of the Church is heard, suggesting the Hymn of St. Patrick
or of a Litany.) Enter St. Patrick with Crossbearer and Attendants. Duffach
alone rises to greet him; the others remain as before.*

PATRICK   A blessing on all here! To thee, O King,
             And to all Erin under thy command
             I bring a greeting and a solemn message
             From Him I serve, my Monarch and my King.

141

LAERE
Thou art a herald, then, and not a priest!
Who is thy monarch, and what embassy
Bring'st thou to us?

DOGHRA
The stranger speaks in figures.
His monarch is the God whom he adores.

CRUDO
His coming heralds strife and war and death!

PATRICK
My message is of peace and bliss to all,
Of Happiness that Heaven alone can give.
My monarch is my God, the King of Heaven,
He is the King of Kings, the Lord of lords;
Nor is this voice a stranger to your hearts;
In ages past your fathers heard his words,
But in the distant wanderings of the Gael
You have forgot his name; His voice
Still moves your hearts to virtue, pity, justice.
Now God has spoken since your fathers' time
Through many mighty prophets, and has sent
His Son from Heaven — Christ — Whose holy name
I now proclaim to you, Who lived and died
That we might learn to live, and after life
To bring to Heaven on high, the good who trust
His name and power. Hither I now come
To summon back the children of the Gael
To hear the voice of God and learn His law.

LAERE
Hast thou thyself beheld these mighty prophets
Or Christ thou speakest of, or known their power?

PATRICK
Hast thou, O King, seen Cormac, son of Art,
Who lived and ruled in Tara? Hast thou known
MacNessa, King of Ulster? Hast thou seen
Those Alpine hills that saw King Dathi die?

LAERE
We have not known these kings, nor have we seen
The snowy Alps, but witnesses of credit
And records duly kept give full assurance
As eye or ear can give.

PATRICK
Hear then, O Kings:
The snowy summits of the Alps look down
On Italy, and point to distant Rome;
When Conor son of Nessa ruled in Ulster
There came to Rome the very witnesses
Who lived with Christ and saw this godly power,
His death and His return unto Heaven;
Who held, besides, the records of the past.

142

These records and the words of witnesses
Transmitted to our times are firm proof
Of all the truths which I will now unfold
Unless your Druids fear to hear the truth.

CRUDO   Thou canst not, impious stranger, prove those things
Thou wouldst forbid the worship which we pay
To sun and moon and sacred stars of heaven;
Thou wouldst, instead, teach us thy mysteries,
For I have stood in mighty Rome itself
And heard from Christian teachers that thy God
Is one and also three — three Gods — not one —
Impossible for mind to understand.

PATRICK   The sun and moon and shining stars above
But point the way unto the highest heavens;
They are the footstool of the lofty throne
Of God invisible; they, like brilliant heralds,
Speak to us of the King and hear this message.
Say, thou, Malathna, if a royal herald
Doth come to Tara's gates, does he receive
The honour of a King?

MALATHNA   The honours of a herald are his due.
To give him more dishonours every king.

PATRICK   And 'tis dishonour to the King of Heaven
To honour as a god the brilliant lights
Announcing but the glory and the power
Of Him who rules and moves them in their paths.
The Druid speaks of Christian mysteries,
But let him first explain the prophecy
of Druids' oracles, by heaven permitted,
Foretelling future triumphs of the Gael
Beyond the seas. Where are the promised triumphs?
Whence and when came the Druids?
You cannot tell. Then listen; Erin's sons
Shall conquer not by war nor sword nor spear,
But by this sacred standard of the cross
Which they shall bear from bleak Iona's strand
To distant Appenine and by the power
Of God, one only God, but one in Three.

CRUDO   'One God, but three in One.' What earthly mind
Can comprehend such things? They cannot be!

PATRICK   What mind can comprehend how nature works?
But still she works, unfolding leaf and flower;
How can a little seed contain the essence

143

Of root and trunk and branch, and leaf and flower;
Behold this shamrock growing at our feet
Ready to give an answer to thy question,
For three in one and one in three, its leaves
Extend o'er all the land. So shall the faith
In triune God extend through Inisfail,
And Erin's sons the shamrock shall exalt
And take its very colour for its banners
Where'er their footsteps lead throughout the earth.
Princes and royal ladies here assembled.
If you would learn the truth I come to teach
Come with me, for upon the plain beneath
The people wait to hear the joyous words
Their souls do hunger for.

CRUDO *to*   Beware, O King,
LAERE   And go not with the stranger priest.

ETHNA   Patrick, we come.

DUFFACH   We follow thee (Eoghan) to hear thee (Mor) and to believe.

(*Exit Patrick and attendants followed by everyone except the Druids, who keep back Laere.*)

Notes

1899

1 Edmund Curtis, *A History of Ireland* (London: Methuen & Co. Ltd., 1950), p. 388.

2 Æ, 'The Dramatic Treatment of Heroic Literature', in *Samhain: An Occasional Review Edited by W. B. Yeats* (Dublin: Sealy Bryers & Walker; London: T. Fisher Unwin, 1902), p. 11.

3 *Ibid.*, p. 12.

4 Ernest A. Boyd, *Ireland's Literary Renaissance* (Dublin & London: Maunsel & Co. Ltd., 1916), pp. 94-95.

5 Colman's verses were spoken by Mr. Farren on 19 January 1821, at the opening of the Theatre Royal. They were printed in *The Dublin Evening Post* for 21 January 1821, and they were reprinted in a four-page pamphlet issued by the theatre of its re-opening on 13 December 1897. A copy of the pamphlet is to be found in the National Library of Ireland.

6 Hamilton's address is printed on pp. 1-2 of the pamphlet mentioned above.

7 Frank J. Fay, 'Irish Drama at the Theatre Royal', *The United Irishman* (8 July 1899); reprinted in *Towards a National Theatre: The Dramatic Criticism of Frank J. Fay*, ed. Robert Hogan (Dublin: The Dolmen Press, 1970), p. 18.

8 Frank J. Fay, 'Irish Drama at the Theatre Royal', *The United Irishman* (29 July 1899); reprinted in *Towards a National Theatre*, p. 20.

9 After an earlier appearance in the provinces, *Charley's Aunt* was presented in London in December, 1892, and had an initial run of four years. *The Oxford Companion to the Theatre* (3rd edition) remarks that the play 'has figured in the repertory of almost every amateur and provincial theatre, as well as being played all over the world in English and in innumerable translations. At one time it was running simultaneously in 48 theatres in 22 languages, among them Afrikaans, Chinese, Esperanto, Gaelic, Russian, and Zulu.' In the most recent revival we have seen of the play in Dublin, by Illsley and McCabe at the Olympia, it opened on St. Stephen's Day in 1962, and played for a month to crowded houses, in a theatre with a capacity of about 1500.

10 Bernard Shaw, *Our Theatres in the Nineties*, Vol. II (London: Constable & Co. Ltd., 1932), p. 172.

11 Fagan was born in 1873 in Belfast, and was at various times in his career an actor, a playwright, and a distinguished producer. His acting

career began in 1895 with the Benson Company, and he played from 1897 to 1899 with Tree. *The Rebels* was followed by — to mention only his most successful pieces — *The Prayer of the Sword* of 1904 in five acts and prose and verse, *The Earth* of 1913, *Doctor O'Toole* of 1917, his Pepysian comedy *And So To Bed* of 1926, and *The Improper Duchess* of 1931. He also wrote successful dramatizations of *Treasure Island* and of Hawthorne's *Wonder Tales*. As a producer, he was notable for forming the Oxford Playhouse in 1923 and becoming a director of the Festival Theatre, Cambridge, in 1929. His more notable London productions included Brieux's *Damaged Goods* in 1917, various Shakespeare productions, *The Government Inspector* in 1920, *The Cherry Orchard* in 1925, and *The Spook Sonata* in 1927. He managed the Irish Players and produced many of their plays. Among the Irish plays he brought to London were O'Casey's *Juno and the Paycock* and *The Plough and the Stars*, Lennox Robinson's *The Whiteheaded Boy*, and George Shiels's *Professor Tim*.

12 Joseph Holloway, *Impressions of a Dublin Playgoer* (24 September 1895). This is a vast manuscript journal housed in the National Library of Ireland. It covers a period of about fifty-six years, from the late 1880's to the early 1940's, and is approximately 25,000,000 words long. A selection of the years from 1899 to 1926 has been edited by Robert Hogan and Michael J. O'Neill and published under the title of *Joseph Holloway's Abbey Theatre* (Carbondale: Southern Illinois University Press, 1967). See also a further selection, from 1926 until Holloway's death: *Joseph Holloway's Irish Theatre*, 1926-1931 (Dixon, California: Proscenium Press, 1968); 1932-1937 (1969); and 1938-1944 (1970).

13 *Ibid.*, 15 September 1896.

14 *Ibid.*, 6 October 1896.

15 *Ibid.*, 4 May 1897.

16 *Ibid.*, 29 June 1897.

17 *Ibid.*, 9 November 1897.

18 Holloway actually wrote 'unsensible', which is no doubt also apt, but probably not what he intended.

19 *Ibid.*, 21 December 1897.

20 *Ibid.*, 3 August 1898.

21 *Ibid.*, 9 August 1898.

22 *Ibid.*, 3 November 1898.

23 Frank J. Fay, ' "Wolfe Tone" at the Queen's Theatre', *The United Irishman*, (26 August 1899), p. 5.

24 Frank J. Fay, ' "The Irishman" at the Queen's Theatre', *The United Irishman*, (9 September 1899), p. 5.

25 Frank J. Fay, ' "The Green Bushes" at the Queen's Theatre', *The United Irishman*, (16 September 1899), p. 5.

26 Holloway, *Impressions*, 13 August 1895.

27 *Ibid.*, 7 September 1898.

28 From the programme of 15 November 1897, contained in a small bound volume of Olympia Theatre Programmes, 1896-1946, housed in the National Library of Ireland.

29 Frank J. Fay, 'Irish Drama at the Theatre Royal', *The United Irishman*, (8 July 1899), p. 1.

30 W. G. Fay and Catherine Carswell, *The Fays of the Abbey Theatre*, (New York: Harcourt, Brace & Co., 1935), p. 71.

31 Nevertheless, the group did get plenty of practice. W. A. Henderson gives what is probably not a complete list of the group's activities in 1899. On 2 January they played at the Coffee Palace in Townsend Street; on 3 and 4 January at the Textonion Bazaar; on 21 January at the Dalkey People's Concerts; on 6 February at the Coffee Palace; on 17 March at the Workmen's Club in York Street, when Frank Fay gave some readings; on 1 May at the Coffee Palace, when they presented *Round the Corner*; on 2 and 3 May at St. Teresa's Hall; on 13 May at the Town Hall in Dalkey; on 16 October at the Coffee Palace; on 25 and 26 October at St. Teresa's Hall, when they presented four different plays; on 19 October at the Rathmines Town Hall; on 8 December at Adelaide Road Presbyterian Church, when Frank Fay gave a reading; on 18 December at the Coffee Palace, when they gave two plays and Dudley Digges gave a recitation. Henderson Ms. 1729, National Library of Ireland.

32 Holloway, *Impressions*, 3 December 1897.

33 George Fitzmaurice, 'Maeve's Grand Lover', *The Irish Weekly Independent and Nation* (17 November 1900), p. 6.

34 Mary Costello, 'A Daughter to Marry', *The Lady of the House*, (Christmas, 1900), pp. 49-50, 53-54.

35 George Moore, *Hail and Farewell : Ave* (London: William Heinemann, 1911), p. 43.

36 W. B. Yeats, 'I Became an Author', *The Listener* (4 August 1938), p. 217.

37 Joseph Hone, *W. B. Yeats, 1865-1939* (London: The Macmillan Co., 1960), p. 107.

38 Alan Wade, ed., *The Letters of W. B. Yeats* (London: Rupert Hart-Davis, 1954), p. 231.

147

39 Lady Gregory, *Our Irish Theatre* (London & New York: G. P. Putnam's Sons, 1913), pp. 8-9.

40 Denis Gwynn, *Edward Martyn and the Irish Revival* (London: Jonathan Cape, 1930), pp. 125-127.

41 Letter of Æ (George W. Russell) to Edward Martyn, quoted in Gwynn, pp. 127-128.

42 From an unsigned review in *The Theatre* (1 April 1893), p. 215.

43 J. T. Grein, *The New World of the Theatre, 1923-1924* (London: Martin Hopkinson & Co., 1924), p. 27.

44 Clifford Bax, ed., *Florence Farr, Bernard Shaw, W. B. Yeats, Letters* (New York: Dodd, Mead & Co.), pp. 21-22.

45 *Ibid.*, p. 23.

46 Moore, *Ave*, p. 91.

47 Wade, *The Letters of W. B. Yeats*, p. 317.

48 Hone, *W. B. Yeats*, p. 169.

49 F. Hugh O'Donnell, *Souls for Gold* (London: Nassau Press, 1899).

50 W. B. Yeats, 'The Irish Literary Theatre', *The Freeman's Journal*, (12 January 1899), p. 5.

51 See letter of W. B. Yeats to Fiona MacLeod (William Sharp), early in 1897, inviting her to submit a play: in Elizabeth Sharp, *William Sharp (Fiona MacLeod)* (London: William Heinemann, 1910), pp. 280-282; reprinted in Yeats's *Letters*, pp. 279-280.

52 Probably W. A. Henderson who was for years the secretary of the National Literary Society, contained in Henderson Ms. 1729, N.L.I.

53 W. B. Yeats, 'Plans and Methods', *Beltaine* (May 1899), pp. 6-9.

54 *Ibid.*

55 James H. and Margaret E. Cousins, *We Two Together* (Madras: Ganesh & Co. Ltd., 1950), p. 56. There is a discrepancy between this report and Moore's account in *Ave* that he was not in Ireland at this time.

56 Editorial, *The Daily Express* (13 May 1899), p. 4.

57 Editorial, *The Daily Nation* (6 May 1899), p. 4.

58 During the week of 8 May, the Irish Literary Theatre had the following competition from the commercial theatres. At the Gaiety, Mr. Herbert Sleath's Company from the Strand Theatre, London, was presenting 'the immensely successful American Farce' *What Happened to Jones* and an unnamed Comedietta. At the Theatre Royal, Mr. C. J. Abud's

148

Company from the Court Theatre, London, was holding the boards with *The Highwayman, Faithful James*, and *A Pantomime Rehearsal*. At the Queen's, Mr. Rollo Balmain's Company was appearing in 'the latest London Dramatic Success', *The Man in the Iron Mask*. The Empire Palace, 'Dublin's Premiere Amusement Palace', was presenting its usual 'Stupendous Attractions' and 'Sparkling Programme'. The feature artiste was Mlle. De Dio in 'She' or the Fire of Life, in which the audience was promised a 'Grand Transition of Youth and Beauty to a realisation of Charred Remains!' This spectacle, presumably suggested by Rider Haggard's novel, contained 'dazzling Electrical Effects' and was alleged to be 'one of the most expensive and Grandest Scenes Ever Witnessed in Dublin'. Among the 'Hosts of Stars' also on the Programme were the Robinson-Baker Trio, who were American scientific trick jumpers; Minnie Cunningham, 'Dublin's Little Idol'; Mr. Leo Dryden, 'Most Legitimate Vocal Actor on the Stage'; Manning and Prevost, comic acrobats; and Tennyson and O'Gorman, 'Leading Irish Comedians . . . (From all Principal London Halls)'. Among the 'Stupendous Attractions' at the Lyric Theatre of Varieties were Captain Devereaux's Company of Canine Comedians, and Les Karsy's Miraculous Myriophone ('The Marvellous Piece of Mechanism Breathes the Very Soul of Music, Specially Engaged for the Great Paris Exhibition of 1900, Now Shown for the first time in Ireland, a Magnificent Treat for the Lover of Music').

59 Cousins, *We Two Together*, p. 57.

60 Robert Hogan and Michael J. O'Neill, eds., *Joseph Holloway's Abbey Theatre* (Carbondale: Southern Illinois University Press, 1967), p. 6.

61 Seumas O'Sullivan, *The Rose and Bottle and Other Essays* (Dublin: The Talbot Press, 1946), pp. 119-120.

62 T. W. Rolleston, Letter, *The Freeman's Journal* (10 May 1899), p. 6.

63 'The Irish Literary Theatre', *The Freeman's Journal* (9 May 1899), p. 5.

64 'The Literary Theatre', *The Daily Express* (9 May 1899) p. 5.

65 Hogan and O'Neill, *Holloway's Abbey Theatre*, p. 7.

66 Michael Cardinal Logue, Letter to Editor, *The Daily Nation* (10 May 1899), p. 5.

67 Frederick Ryan, Letter to Editor, *The Irish Daily Independent* (11 May 1899), p. 3.

68 F. Hugh O'Donnell, 'Bowdlerizing the Countess', *The Daily Nation* (12 May 1899), p. 5.

69 Letter to Editor, *The Daily Nation* (10 May 1899), p. 5.

70 'The Irish Literary Theatre', *The Freeman's Journal* (10 May 1899), p. 5.

71 'The Irish Literary Theatre', *The Irish Times* (10 May 1899), p. 5.

72 Max Beerbohm, 'In Dublin', *The Saturday Review* (13 May 1899), pp. 587-588.

73 Moore, *Ave.*, pp. 94-95.

74 Hogan and O'Neill, *Holloway's Abbey Theatre*, p. 9.

75 'Irish Literary Theatre: Dinner at the Shelbourne Hotel', *The Daily Express* (12 May 1899), pp. 5-6.

76 Alice Milligan (14 September 1865 - 13 April 1953) was throughout her life a student of Irish language and culture. In Belfast she edited the *Shan Van Vocht* and later *The Northern Patriot*, both journals advocating the revival of Irish art and writing and Ireland's separation from England. She wrote several volumes of poetry, as well as a number of plays on Irish history and mythology, the best known of which is *The Last Feast of the Fianna*, produced by the Irish Literary Theatre in 1900. For a charming short reminiscence of her in her old age, see Benedict Kiely's article 'The Whores on the Half-doors' in *Conor Cruise O'Brien Introduces Ireland*, ed. Owen Dudley Edwards (London: Andre Deutsch, 1969), pp. 150-151.

77 'About six weeks ago an anonymous play in four acts about an old Irish story and a musical play with words by a nun, were acted in Letterkenny before enthusiastic audiences.' W. B. Yeats, 'The Irish Literary Theatre', *The Daily Express* (14 January 1899), p. 3. Most of this article was printed in a revised form as 'Plans and Methods', *Beltaine* (May 1899), pp. 6-9.

78 The Irish interlude of this play is printed in Appendix II, with its English translation.

79 Alice Milligan, Letter to Editor, *The Daily Express* (21 January 1899), p. 3.

80 'Imtheacht Conaill', *The Freeman's Journal* (19 November 1899), p. 6.

81 'A Gaelic Theatre', *Fainne an Lae* (4 February 1899), pp. 37-38.

82 'The Gaelic League Festival', *The Irish News and Belfast Morning News* (8 May 1898), p. 6.

83 'Tableaux Vivants at the Chief Secretary's Lodge', *The Daily Express* (26 January 1899), p. 5.
    Yesterday evening and on Tuesday evening the Chief Secretary for Ireland and Lady Betty Balfour entertained a limited number of guests with a number of tableaux vivants based on Mr. W. B. Yeats's poetical play, *Countess Cathleen*. The salient points in the tragedy of the noble-hearted Countess were admirably condensed into a series of nine tableaux, commencing with the temptation and fall of Shemus Rua, and ending with a beautiful picture of Cathleen 'passing to the floor in

peace'. The various parts were taken by ladies and gentlemen who were in thorough sympathy with the Celtic inspiration of the poet, and the scenes were simply, yet richly staged. Historical accuracy was observed with regard to the dresses and ornaments, some of which were modelled on actual Celtic specimens preserved in our National Museum. Between, and sometimes during the tableaux the audience was delighted with old Irish songs and instrumental music. None who heard it last night will easily forget the splendidly sorrowful notes of the Celtic 'goll' or 'caoine', which was sung during the passing of the Countess. The striking success of the entertainment was proved by the fact that, although the silent art of the tableau is not the best medium for conveying the influence of a subtle literary atmosphere, last night's pictures were wonderfully effective in interpreting to the spectators something of that impalpable glamour which permeates the best work of Mr. Yeats and his school. To Lady Betty Balfour herself, the daughter and grand-daughter of poets, the prestige of this difficult literary accomplishment is very largely due.

84 'Trinity College and the Literary Theatre', *The Daily Express* (1 June 1899), p. 5.

1900

1 F. J. Fay, 'Pelléas et Mélisande at the Theatre Royal', *The United Irishman* (1 September 1900); reprinted in *Towards a National Theatre*, p. 44.

2 Val Vousden, *Val Vousden's Caravan* (Dublin: Cahill & Co. Ltd., 1941), pp. 13-16.

3 W. B. Yeats, 'The Irish Literary Theatre, 1900'. *Beltaine* (1900), pp. 22-24; reprinted from *The Dome* of January 1900.

4 W. B. Yeats, 'Plans and Methods', *Beltaine* (1900), pp. 3-6.

5 George Moore, 'Is the Theatre a Place of Amusement?', *ibid.*, pp. 7-10.

6 Edward Martyn, 'A comparison between Irish and English Theatrical Audiences', *ibid.*, p. 12.

7 Yeats, *ibid.*, p. 21.

8 Alice Milligan, 'The Last Feast of the Fianna', *ibid.*, pp. 20-21.

9 Lady Gregory, 'Last Year', *ibid.*, pp. 25-26.

10 Joseph Hone, *The Life of George Moore* (London: Victor Gollancz Ltd., 1936), p. 220.

11 Moore, *Ave*, pp. 166-167.

12 *Ibid.*, p. 278.

13 *Ibid.*, p. 284.

14 *Ibid.*, p. 285.

15 Hone, *Moore*, pp. 221-222.

16 'The Irish Literary Theatre', *The Freeman's Journal* (20 February 1900), p. 5.

17 'Irish Literary Theatre', *The Daily Express* (20 February 1900), p. 5.

18 *Ibid.*

19 The 'By the Way' column in *The Freeman's Journal* noted on 21 March 1907, that in this original production of *The Last Feast of the Fianna*, John O'Leary, Yeats's friend and the old Fenian leader, 'favoured the authoress by appearing amongst the band of warriors feasting at the banquet board. His appearance in the robes of a warrior of the ancient Fianna was particularly striking and appropriate, and, as this may have been his only appearance on the stage, it is pleasing to know that a photograph of him was taken as a memento of the occasion.' (p. 8)

In an article, 'Staging and Costume in Irish Drama', published in the 30 March 1904 issue of *Ireland's Own*, Alice Milligan noted that Grania in this production 'wore a rose-coloured sateen robe, dark-blue serge mantle, golden veil and ornaments'. She also remarked that the character of Niamh on this occasion 'wore a pale-green clinging robe, with silver lustre scarf and girdle, strings of pearl and iridescent shells, and a veil of filmy chiffon, clasped with a silver fillet'. And finally she remarked: 'I am here bound to confess as a dreadful warning to others that at *The Last Feast of the Fianna* in the Gaiety Theatre I forgot to arrange the bill of fare. There was not a scrap of food of any sort on the board in consequence.' (pp. 6-7)

20 'Irish Literary Theatre', *The Irish Daily Independent* (20 February 1900), p. 6.

21 'The Irish Literary Theatre', *The Irish Times* (20 February 1900), p. 6.

22 'The Irish Literary Theatre', *The Freeman's Journal* (21 February 1900), p. 5.

23 'Irish Literary Theatre', *The Irish Daily Independent* (21 February 1900), p. 5.

24 'Irish Literary Theatre', *The Daily Express* (21 February 1900), p. 5.

25 Holloway, *Impressions*, 20 February 1900, Ms. 1798, N.L.I.

26 'The Irish Literary Theatre', *The Irish Times* (21 February, 1900), p. 6.

27 James Cousins in *We Two Together* wrote: 'There were rumours that its authorship was either a composite affair or a plagiarism; and some confirmation of one or other of the rumours appeared to be found later when Mr. Martyn published *The Tale of a Town*. Both plays, it was whispered, were pilfered from Æ who told the original story to both Moore and Martyn.' (pp. 57-58)

28 'The Irish Literary Theatre', *The Irish Daily Independent* (22 February 1900), p. 4.

29 'The Irish Literary Theatre', *The Freeman's Journal* (23 February 1900), p. 6.

30 'Robert Emmet', *The United Irishman* (17 November 1900), p. 7.

31 Letters to Alice L. Milligan, Ms. 5048, National Library of Ireland.

32 *Ibid.*

33 'Dedication of St. Margaret's', *The Freeman's Journal* (26 November 1900), p. 5.

1901

1 'Inghinidhe na hEireann, Gaelic Tableaux Vivants', *The Freeman's Journal* (10 April 1901), p. 5.

2 Holloway, Impressions, 10 April 1901. Ms. 1799, N.L.I.

3 'Inghinidhe na hEireann, A Successful Entertainment', *The Freeman's Journal* (26 August 1901), p. 6. Miss Milligan's play was referred to by Dudley Digges as '*The Harp That Once* (and only once, thank God)'. Quoted in Fay and Carswell, p. 68.

4 'Gaelic Tableaux', *The Irish Daily Independent and Nation* (28 August 1901), p. 5.

5 P. T. MacGinley was an enthusiastic Gaelic Leaguer who at this time wrote three short plays which were published under the auspices of the Gaelic League. *Eilis agus an Bhean Deirce* has been translated into English and published under the title of *Lizzie and the Tinker*, in the collection *Lost Plays of the Irish Renaissance*, eds. Hogan and Kilroy (Dixon, California: Proscenium Press, 1970).

6 George Moore, *Ave*, p. 354.

7 George Moore, *Salve* (London: William Heinemann, 1912), p. 107.

8 *Ibid.*, p. 106.

9 Letter of George Moore to Douglas Hyde, written on 17 September 1901, in the possession of Robert Hogan. The correspondence referred to was prompted by a *Freeman's Journal* interview with George Moore on the question of why Elgar, rather than an Irish composer, was chosen. Summarized by the *Freeman*, his answer was: 'Because George Moore does not know any Irish musician who can write for orchestra except one in Paris, who is not available.' 'The Irish Literary Theatre', *The Freeman's Journal* (13 September 1901), p. 3.

10 Fay and Carswell, pp. 114-115.

11 Quoted in Hogan and O'Neill, *Holloway's Abbey Theatre*, p. 34.

12 Quoted in J. C. Trewin, *Benson and the Bensonians* (London: Barrie and Rockliff, 1960), p. 129.

13 Quoted in Lady Gregory, *Our Irish Theatre*, pp. 28-29.

14 Trewin, pp. 130-131.

15 W. B. Yeats, 'Windlestraws', *Samhain* (1901), p. 10. *Beltaine* was the old name for May, beginning of summer. It and Samhain were the two great feasts of the Celtic year. This passage is also to be found in *Explorations* (London, 1962), p. 84.

16 *Ibid.*, p. 9.

17 Footnote by W. B. Yeats: 'I do not want dramatic blank verse to be chanted, as people understand that word, but I do not want actors to speak as prose what I have taken much trouble to write as verse. Lyrical verse is another matter, and that I hope to hear spoken to musical notes in some theatre some day.'

18 George Moore, 'The Irish Literary Theatre', *Samhain* (1901), pp. 11-13.

19 Edward Martyn, 'A Plea for a National Theatre in Ireland', *Samhain* (1901), pp. 14-15.

20 Standish James O'Grady (1846-1928) was at this time the editor of the *All-Ireland Review*. In addition to his work mentioned in the chapter '1899', his trilogy, composed of *The Coming of Cuchulain, The Gates of the North* and *The Fall of Cuchulain*, gave also a fictionalized version of Celtic legends. See Hugh Art O'Grady's *Standish James O'Grady: The Man and the Writer* (Dublin and Cork: The Talbot Press Ltd., 1929), and Phillip L. Marcus, *Standish O'Grady* (Lewisburg: Bucknell University Press, 1970).

21 Standish O'Grady, 'The Story of Diarmid and Grania', *All-Ireland Review* (19 October 1901), p. 244.

22 George Moore was not, Yeats announced from the stage, in the house. However, in *Salve*, Moore writes that, although he had originally intended not to go, Frank Fay persuaded him to.

23 'The Irish Literary Theatre', *The Freeman's Journal* (22 October 1901), p. 4.

24 'Gaiety Theatre: The Irish Literary Theatre', *The Irish Times* (22 October 1901), p. 4.

25 'The Irish Theatre', *The Irish Daily Independent and Nation* (22 October 1901), p. 5.

26 M.A.M., 'Too Much Grania', *The Evening Herald* (22 October 1901), p. 2.

27 Frank J. Fay, 'The Irish Literary Theatre', *The United Irishman* (26 October 1901), p. 2; reprinted in *Towards a National Theatre*, p. 73.

28 Frank J. Fay, 'The Irish Literary Theatre', *The United Irishman* (2 November 1901), p. 2; reprinted in *Towards a National Theatre*, pp. 77-78.

29 *Ibid.*

30 'By the Way', *The Freeman's Journal* (24 October 1901), p. 4.

31 A typed article attributed to Cousins by W. A. Henderson, and contained in Henderson Ms. 1729, N.L.I.

32 Cousins, *We Two Together*, pp. 62-63.

155

33 'By the Way', *The Freeman's Journal* (24 October 1901), p. 4.

34 James Joyce, 'The Day of the Rabblement', *The Critical Writings of James Joyce,* eds. Ellsworth Mason and Richard Ellmann (London: Faber and Faber, 1959), p. 70.

35 *Ibid.,* p. 71.

36 *Ibid.,* pp. 71-72.

37 Frank J. Fay, 'The Irish Literary Theatre', *The United Irishman* (2 November 1901), p. 2; reprinted in *Towards a National Theatre,* p. 79.

38 Stephen Gwynn, 'The Irish Literary Theatre and its Affinities', *The Fortnightly Review* (1901), pp. 1055-58.

39 *Ibid.,* pp. 1058-59.

40 *Ibid.,* p. 1062.

41 Percy M. Young, *Elgar* (London: Collins, 1955), pp. 96-97.

42 *Ibid.,* p. 355.

43 John F. Porte, *Elgar and his Music* (London: Sir Isaac Pitman and Sons Ltd., 1933), pp. 86-87.

44 W. H. Reed, *Elgar* (London: J. M. Dent & Sons, Ltd., 1949), p. 64.

45 F. R. Benson, *My Memoirs* (London: Ernest Benn Ltd., 1930), p. 311.

46 *Ibid.*

47 'Irial' [Fred Ryan], 'Has the Irish National Theatre Failed?' *The United Irishman* (9 November 1901), p. 3.

48 'The Irish Literary Theatre, Interview with Mr. George Moore', *The Freeman's Journal* (13 November 1901), p. 5.

49 'Sacerdos', letter in *The Freeman's Journal* (14 November 1901), p. 4.

50 George Moore, letter to Editor in *The Freeman's Journal* (14 November 1901), p. 4.

51 W. B. Yeats, letter to Editor in *The Freeman's Journal* (15 November 1901), p. 4. Reprinted in Yeats's *Letters,* pp. 356-357.

52 George Moore, letter in *The Freeman's Journal* (16 November 1901), p. 5.

53 *Ibid.*

54 Max Beerbohm, *Around Theatres* (London: Rupert Hart-Davis, 1952), pp. 60-61.

Index

Abbey Theatre, 78.
The Adoration of the Magi (W. B. Yeats), 111.
Advice Gratis (C. Dance), 22.
Alexander, George, 10, 77.
Allgood, Sara, 21.
The All-Ireland Review, 101.
Antony and Cleopatra (Shakespeare), 11.
Arrah-na-Pogue (Dion Boucicault), 11, 12, 19.
Archer, William, 121.
Arliss, George, 89.
Arms and the Man (G. B. Shaw), 24-25, 28.
Arnold, Somerfield, 11.
As You Like It (Shakespeare), 11.

The Bandit King, 14.
Bards of the Gall and Gaul (G. Sigerson), 9.
Barr, Herbert, 15-16.
Barrie, J. M., 11.
The Beaux Stratagem (G. Farquhar), 37.
Beerbohm, Max, 48, 51. Quoted 47, 130.
Behan, Brendan, 17.
The Belle of New York (H. Morton), 11.
The Bells (L. D. Lewis), 89.
Beltaine, 34, 65-68.
The Bending of the Bough (G. Moore), 28, 65, 70, 75-79, 84, 99-100, 127,
    134.
Benson, Mrs. F. R., 103, 105, 117.
Benson, F. R., 11, 13, 92, 95-96, 102, 103, 107, 110, 115. Quoted 117.
Cyrano de Bergerac (E. Rostand), 13.
Bernhardt, Sarah, 13, 29.
The Bohemian Girl (A. Bunn), 11.
Borthwick, Norma, 53.
Boucicault, Dion, 11-12, 17, 19, 21.
Boyd, St. Clair, 56.
Boyd, Ernest, 8. Quoted 9.
Box and Cox (J. M. Morton), 22.
Breen, Frank, 21.
Bryden, Ronald, 17.
Brydon, Alfred, 103.
Buchanan, Robert, 10.
Buckstone, John B., 18, 22.
Bulwer-Lytton, Edward, 11.

Calderon, Pedro, 35, 36.
Cahill, Agnes, 74-75.
Callanan, Jeremiah J., 35.
Camille (A. Dumas *fils*), 11.
Campbell, Mrs. Patrick, 11, 61, 78, 89, 103.
Carleton, William, 8.
Carte, D'Oyle, Company, 13, 61.
Casadh an tSugáin or *The Twisting of the Rope* (D. Hyde), 92-95, 96,
    102-103, 107, 136.
Celibates (G. Moore), 112.

The Celtic Twilight (W. B. Yeats), 9.
Charley's Aunt (B. Thomas), 13, 61, 71, 123, 145n.
The Children of Lir (P. Colum), 135.
Clarke, Austin, 130.
Coffey, Mrs. George, 33.
The Colleen Bawn (Dion Boucicault), 11, 12, 64.
Collier, Jeremy, 37.
Colman the Younger, Quoted 9-10.
Comédie Française, 124.
A Comedy of Sighs (J. Todhunter), 9, 24, 28.
The Coming of Conall (Sr. M. Gertrude), 54.
Compton, Edward, 13, 14.
Congreve, William, 37.
Cooke, Fred, 18-19.
Coquelin, Benoit Constant, 13.
The Corsician Brothers (Dion Boucicault), 107.
Costello, Mary, 23.
The Countess Cathleen (W. B. Yeats), 9, 26, 29-34, 35, 36-45, 49-52, 64, 68, 70, 97-100, 127, 133.
The Country Wife (W. Wycherley), 37.
La Course du Flambeau (P. Hervieu), 89.
Cousins, James H., Quoted 36-37, 39, 108-110.
Creadeamh agus Gorta (Fr. Dinneen), 97.
Curtis, Edmund, Quoted 8.

The Daily Express, 34, 45, 47, 52. Quoted 37-38, 41-42, 48, 58-60, 71-72, 76-77, 150-151.
The Daily Mail, Quoted 47, 48.
The Daily Nation, 43, 44. Quoted 38-39.
The Daily Telegraph, Quoted 48.
Dalton, Frank, 12, 21.
D'Annunzio, Gabriele, 112.
Darcy, Fred, 15.
The Daughter of the Regiment, 11.
A Daughter to Mary (M. Costello), 23-24.
Daughters of Erin (Inghinidhe na hEireann), 85, 89-91, 100.
'The Day of the Rabblement' (J. Joyce). Quoted 111-112.
Deirdre (Æ), 85.
The Deliverance of Red Hugh (A. Milligan), 91, 135.
Devereux, William, 77.
The Devil's Disciple (G. B. Shaw), 61.
Diarmuid and Grania (G. Moore and W. B. Yeats), 81, 92, 93, 95-96, 100, 102-117, 119, 127, 129, 135-136.
Digges, Dudley, 21.
Dinneen, Fr., 120, 125.
The Dome, 34.
Drink (Charles Reade), 14.
The Dublin University Review, 24.
Dumas, Alexandre, *fils*, 11.
du Maurier, George, 89.

East Lynne (T. A. Palmer), 62.
The Echo, Quoted 47.
Edgeworth, Maria, 8.
Edwardes, George Company, 13.
Edwin, T. Bryant, 71, 72.

Eglinton, John (W. K. Magee), 48.
Eilis agus an Bhean Deirce (P. T. Mac Ginley), 91, 97, 135.
Elgar, Edward, 108, 115-117, 154n.
Ellis, Harrold and Paul A. Rubens, 11.
Ellmann, Richard, 111.
The Enchanted Sea (E. Martyn), 125.
An Enemy of the People (H. Ibsen), 78.
Ervine, St. John, Quoted 28-29.
Esther Waters (G. Moore), 27, 78, 112.
Evelyn Innes (G. Moore), 111.
The Evening Herald, Quoted 43, 46, 105-106.

Fagan, James B., 13-14, 145-146n.
Fáinne an Lae, Quoted 55-56.
The Family Speaker, 23.
Farquhar, George, 37.
Farr, Florence, 24, 28-30, 40, 42.
Fay, Frank, 78, 85, 129. Quoted 11-12, 18, 21, 61, 95, 106-108, 112-113.
Fay, W. G., 21-22, 78, 85, 91, 96, 129. Quoted 22, 94-95.
Ferguson, Sir Samuel, 8, 60, 84.
Fitzmaurice, George, Quoted 23.
Flaubert, Gustave, 112.
Flint, McHardy, 21.
The Football King (G. Gray), 15-16.
The Fortnightly Review, 113.
Franklein, Lucy, 103.
The Freeman's Journal, 31, 33, 94. Quoted 40-41, 45-46, 54-55, 70-71, 75, 90-91, 102-104, 110-111, 119-125, 126, 129.
Frith, Walter, 10.

Gaelic League, 9, 53-54, 56, 81, 100, 114, 129.
The Gaiety, 13, 61, 70, 71, 78, 89, 92, 96, 99, 102, 115, 129.
Gertrude, Sister Mary, 54.
Gill, T. P. Quoted 48-49.
Gogarty, Oliver St. John, 130.
Goldberg, Max, 16.
Goldsmith, Oliver, 14.
Gonne, Maud, 85, 89, 102.
Gray, George, 15-16.
A Greek Slave (O. Hall), 11.
The Green Bushes (J. B. Buckstone), 18.
The Green Upon the Cape (A. Milligan), 132.
Gregory, Lady Augusta, 25-26, 30, 69, 82, 92, 95, 96, 114. Quoted 25, 68.
Grein, J. T., 27-28.
Gringoire (T. de Banville), 114.
Gwynn, Stephen, Quoted 113, 114.

Hail and Farewell (G. Moore), 27, 28, 92. Quoted 93.
Hamilton, Edwin, Quoted 10.
Hamlet (Shakespeare), 61.
Hammond, Dorothy, 72, 74.
The Harp That Once (A. Milligan), 90-91, 135.
Hauptmann, Gerrhart, 111.
The Heather Field (Edward Martyn), 26, 33, 34, 45-51, 68-69, 70-71, 97-98, 100, 125, 133.
Henderson, W. A., 33.

159

Herford, C. H., 34.
Hill-Mitchelson, E. and Charles H. Longdon, 16.
His Last Legs (W. B. Bernard), 22.
History of Ireland : Cuculain and His Contemporaries (S. O'Grady), 8.
History of Ireland : The Heroic Period (S. O'Grady), 8-9.
Holloway, Joseph, 95, 146n. Quoted 14-17, 19, 22, 34, 40, 43, 48, 77-78, 89-90.
Hone, Joseph, Quoted 25, 31, 68.
Horniman, A. E. F., 24.
The Hostage (B. Behan), 17.
Hugo, Victor, 51.
Humanity (C. Locksley), 16-17.
Hyde, Douglas, 9, 48, 53, 80, 83, 85, 92-95, 96, 100, 102-104, 107, 114, 119, 123-124.

Ibsen, Henrik, 28, 65, 111, 121.
Ideas of Good and Evil (W. B. Yeats), 34.
Il Fuoco (G. D'Annunzio), 112.
Independent Theatre, 27-28, 34.
The Irish Daily Independent, 43. Quoted 46, 72, 75-76, 79, 91, 104.
An Irish Gentleman (D. C. Murray), 11.
Irish Language, 52-53, 81, 82-84, 90-91, 92-95, 102-104, 107, 112, 129.
Irish Literary Society of London, 9.
'The Irish Literary Theatre' (W. B. Yeats), 65.
The Irishman (J. W. Whitbread), 18.
Irish National Theatre Society, 21, 43, 117.
The Irish News and *Belfast Morning News*, Quoted 56-58.
The Irish Times, 45, 79, 94. Quoted 46-47, 73-75, 78-79, 104.
The Irish Tutor (R. Butler), 22, 85.
Irving, Henry, 89.
The Island of Statues (W. B. Yeats), 24.

Jacobsen, Jens Peter, 112.
Jeannie Deans (C. H. Hazlewood), 12.
Jim, The Penman (C. L. Young), 61.
Johnson, Lionel, 34, 36.
Johnston, Denis, 130.
Jones, Henry Arthur, 13.
Joyce, James, 40, 45, 111, 113. Quoted 111-112.
Juno and the Paycock (S. O'Casey), 17.

Kathleen ni Houlihan (W. B. Yeats), 85.
Kavanagh, Rose, 9.
Kickham, Charles J., 8.
King Lear (Shakespeare), 102.
The King of Friday's Men (M. J. Molloy), 17.
Kingston, Thomas, 46, 68.
Kipling, Rudyard, 52.
Kitty Grey, 123.

The Lady of the House, 23.
The Lady of the Lake, 12.
The Lady of Lyons (E. Bulwer-Lytton), 11.
The Lake (G. Moore), 129.
The Land of Heart's Desire (W. B. Yeats), 9, 24, 28, 83, 132.
Lang, Matheson, 96.

Larminie, William, 50.
The Last Feast of the Fianna (A. Milligan), 67, 70-74, 80, 118, 133-134.
Lawson, John, 16-17.
The Laying of the Foundations (F. Ryan), 117.
Lecky, W. E. H., 26.
The Lily of Killarney (J. Oxenford and D. Boucicault), 11.
The Limerick Boy (J. Pilgrim), 22.
Literary History of Ireland (D. Hyde), 9.
The Little Minister (J. M. Barrie), 11, 61.
Little Miss Nobody (H. Graham), 11.
Little Red Riding Hood, 14.
Lipton, Sir Thomas, 124.
Locksley, Charles, 16-17.
The Love Songs of Connacht (D. Hyde), 9.
Logue, Michael Cardinal, 31, 39, 49-50. Quoted 43.
Lyndal, Percy, 77.
The Lyons Mail (*Courier of Lyons*) (C. Reade), 89.

MacCarthy, Denis Florence, 35.
MacGinley, P. T., 55, 154n.
Mackay, Charles, 21.
'MacLeod, Fiona' (see William Sharp).
MacLiammóir, Micheál, 130.
Madame Bovary (G. Flaubert), 112.
Maeterlinck, Maurice, 65, 77.
Maeve (E. Martyn), 65, 68-69, 70-74, 80, 97, 99, 133.
Magda (L. N. Parker), 11.
Magee, W. K. (see John Eglinton).
The Man of Forty (Walter Firth), 10.
Mangan, James Clarence, 8.
Moody Manners Opera Company, 11.
The Manoeuvres (H. A. Jones), 13.
Mariana (Echegaray), 89.
Martyn, Edward, 24, 25-28, 30, 31, 33, 45-51, 54, 64-65, 82, 84, 87, 92, 96, 99, 111, 121, 125, 127-128. Quoted 66-67, 68-74, 100-101.
Matthews, E. C., 11-12.
Mayeur, Eugene, 77.
The Merchant of Venice (Shakespeare), 89.
Midsummer Night's Dream (Shakespeare), 65.
Miller, Kennedy, 19.
Milligan, Alice, 55, 56, 84, 85, 90-91, 150n, 152-153n. Quoted 52-54, 67.
Milligan-Fox, C., 72.
Molloy, M. J., 17.
Mollison, William, 12.
Moore, George, 27-28, 30, 33, 34, 36-37, 47, 48, 64, 75-79, 81, 84, 92, 95-96, 101, 102-118, 125-130. Quoted 24, 29-30, 51-52, 65-66, 68-70, 93-94, 95, 97-100, 115, 118-125, 126-127, 128.
Morrell, H. H., 10.
Morris, Fanny, 72.
Mosada (W. B. Yeats), 24.
Mouillot, Frederick, 10.
Murray, David Christie, 11.
Murray, Thomas E., 13.
Musset, Alfred de, 114.

National Literary Society, 9, 33, 80-85.
Nerney, Tom, 12.

New Theatre Royal, 9-12.
The New World (F. Darcy), 15.
The Notorious Mrs. Ebbsmith (A. W. Pinero), 11.

O'Byrne, Patrick, 54-55.
O'Casey, Sean, 17, 30, 130.
O'Connor, Frank, 130.
O'Donnell, F. Hugh, 31-33, 43. Quoted 31-33, 44-45.
O'Donoghue, Tadhg, 92.
O'Faolain, Sean, 130.
O'Grady, Standish, 8-9, 33, 35, 48, 106, 111, 155n. Quoted 101.
O'Growney, Fr. Eugene, 54.
O'Heynes, Maeve, 74.
Oisin and Padraic (A. Milligan), 134.
Oisin in Tri-Nan-Oig (A. Milligan), 134.
O'Kennedy, Miss, 93.
Oldham, Edith, 34.
O'Leary, John, 25, 48, 152n.
O'Leary, Fr. P., 119-120, 125.
Olympia Theatre, 20-21.
The Only Way (F. Wills), 11.
On Shannon's Shore (F. Cooke), 18-19.
One of the Bravest, 14.
O'Shea, C. J., 57.
O'Sullivan, Seumas, Quoted, 40
Othello (Shakespeare), 61,89.
Our Irish Visitors, 13.

Paddy Miles (J. Pilgrim), 22.
Paget, Dorothy, 34.
La Parisienne (Henri Becque), 89.
Parnell, C. S., 8, 31.
The Passing of Conall (E. O'Growney), 52, 54, 132.
Pelléas and Mélisande (M. Maeterlinck), 61, 78.
Pettitt, Henry and Sir Augustus Harris, 11.
Pinero, Arthur Wing, 13, 21.
'Plans and Methods' (W. B. Yeats), 34, 65.
The Playboy of the Western World (J. M. Synge), 17, 30.
The Plough and the Stars (S. O'Casey), 30.
Poems and Ballads of Young Ireland, 9.
Porte, John F. Quoted, 116.
Les Précieuses Ridicules (Moliere), 13.
The Prodigal Daughter (H. Pettitt and A. Harris), 11.

Queen's Royal Theatre, 14-20.
Quinn, Maire. Quoted, 85-86.

Reade, Charles, 14.
The Rebels (J. B. Fagan), 13-14.
Reed, W. H. Quoted, 116.
Rehan, Ada, 12.
Réjane, [Madame], 89.
Robert Emmet (R. Pilgrim), 85.
Robertson, Forbes, 61, 89.
Robinson, Lennox, Quoted, 8.
Rob Roy MacGregor (I. Pocock), 12.

162

Rodney, Frank, 103, 107.
Rogers, Brendan J., 54.
Rolleston, T. W., 9. Quoted 40.
Les Romanesques (E. Rostand), 61.
Rosmersholm (H. Ibsen), 28.
Rostand, Edmond, 13.
A Rough Diamond (J. B. Buckstone), 22.
A Runaway Girl (Sir S. Hicks and H. Nichols), 13, 123.
Russell, George (Æ), Quoted 8-9, 26-27.
Russell, T. O'Neill, 54, 56.
Ryan, Frederick, Quoted, 43-44, 117-118.

St. Patrick's Purgatory (P. Calderon), 35.
Salt, Henry, 29.
Samhain, 96-101, 117, 119.
San Toy (E. A. Morton), 61.
Sappho, 89.
Saturday Review, 47.
The School for Scandal (R. B. Sheridan), 11.
The Second Mrs. Tanqueray (A. W. Pinero), 11, 105.
The Secret, 22.
The Secrets of the Harem (M. Goldberg), 16.
The Seeker, (W. B. Yeats), 24.
Shaft No. 2, 15.
Shakespeare, William, 51, 77, 117.
Sharp, William ('Fiona MacLeod'), 33, 35.
The Shaughraun (D. Boucicault), 12, 17.
Shaw, George Bernard, 13, 28, 47. Quoted, 29.
Sheridan, R. B., 14.
The Shop Girl (H. J. W. Dam), 123.
The Siege of Limerick, 64.
Sigerson, George, 9, 33.
The Sign of the Cross, (W. Barrett), 63.
Sims, G. R., 27.
The Skirt Dancer (G. Ridgwell, E. Mansell and R. F. Mackay), 11.
Souls for Gold (F. Hugh O'Donnell), 31-33.
Spencer, Herbert, 105.
The Squatter's Daughter, 11.
The Standard, Quoted, 48.
Starkie, Robert F., 84.
The Strike at Arlingford (G. Moore), 27-28.
Strindberg, August, 111.
Sullivan, Mrs. Charles, 12.
Sweet Nancy (R. Buchanan), 10.
Sweet Nell of Old Drury, 126.
Synge, J. M., 17, 30.

Tadg Saor (P. O'Leary), 97.
The Tale of the Town (E. Martyn), 68, 92, 99, 128.
Tartuffe (Moliere), 13.
The Terror of Paris (E. Hill-Mitchelson), 16.
Terry, Ellen, 89.
That Rascal Pat (J. H. Grover), 22, 85.
'The Theatre' (W. B. Yeats), 34.
Théâtre de L'Oeuvre, 33.
Théâtre Libre, 33, 34.

The Three Musketeers, 13.
The Times (London), Quoted, 48.
An Tobar Draoidheachta (The Magic Well) (Fr. Dinneen), 85.
Todhunter, John, 9, 24, 28.
Tolstoi, Leo, 66.
Topsy-Turvey Hotel (A. Sturgess), 11.
La Tosca (V. Sardou), 13.
The Tragedy of a Simple Soul (M. Costello), 23.
The Trail of the Serpent, 15.
Tree, Herbert Beerbohm, 65, 89.
Trewin, J. C., 96.
Trinity College (Dublin University), 64, 84-85, 100, 123.
Twelfth Night (Shakespeare), 89.
Tynan, Katherine, 9.

The United Irishman, 11-12, 21, 85.
The Untilled Field (G. Moore), 129.

Vain Fortune (G. Moore), 112.
Vousden, Val, Quoted, 61-64.

Waller, Mrs. Lewis, 13.
Walsh, Edward, 35.
Walsh, W., 113, 120, 126, 128. Quoted, 86-87.
Walter, J. Herbert, 72.
The Wanderings of Oisin (W. B. Yeats), 9, 24, 54.
Warner, Charles, 14-15.
Watson, F. Marriot, 15.
The Weekly Freeman, 22.
The Weekly Independent, 22.
West Irish Folk-Tales and Romances (W. Larminie), 50.
Whitbread, J. W., 14, 17.
Whitby, Arthur, 104.
Whitty, May, 30, 42.
Who Speaks First? (C. Dance), 22.
Widowers' Houses (G. B. Shaw), 28.
Williams, Harcourt, 96.
The Wind Among the Reeds (W. B. Yeats), 111.
Wolfe Tone (J. W. Whitbread), 18.
Wycherley, William, 37.

Yeats, W. B., 9, 17, 24-26, 48, 49-52, 54, 58-60, 64, 65, 69, 70, 81, 82, 83, 84, 92, 93, 95, 101, 102-119, 121, 124, 129. Quoted, 9, 24, 25, 30, 33, 34-36, 49-51, 67, 95-96, 97, 115, 126-127.
Young Mr. Yarde (H. Ellis and P. Rubens), 11.
Young, Percy, Quoted, 115-116.

164